Terri Muvanya-Wischmann
"SAFARI PARTNER"

“SAFARI PARTNER”

by Terri Muvanya-Wischmann

Bibliografische Information der Deutschen Bibliothek
Die Deutsche Bibliothek verzeichnet diese Publikation in der Deutschen Nationalbibliografie; detaillierte bibliografische Daten sind im Internet über http://dnb.ddb.de abrufbar.

Terri Muvanya-Wischmann
"SAFARI PARTNER"

Berlin: Pro BUSINESS 2009

ISBN 978-3-86805-235-0

1. Auflage 2009

Produktion und Herstellung: Pro BUSINESS GmbH
Gedruckt auf alterungsbeständigem Papier
Printed in Germany

www.book-on-demand.de

Africa
International Boundary
Road
River
National Capital
City or Town
0 400 1000 KM
0 400 1000 Miles
© 2007 Geology.com
Azores (Portugal)
Madeira Islands (Portugal)
Canary Islands (Spain)
PORTUGAL
SPAIN
ITALY
BULGARIA
Black Sea
GE
AR
AZ
TURKMENISTAN
Caspian Sea
TURKEY
GREECE
CYPRUS
SYRIA
LEBANON
ISRAEL
IRAQ
IRAN
JORDAN
KUWAIT
Persian Gulf
QATAR
U.A.E.
SAUDI ARABIA
OMAN
YEMEN
Gulf of Aden
Red Sea
Mediterranean Sea
Algiers
Annaba
Tunis
Oran
Rabat
Fes
Casablanca
Safi
MOROCCO
Marrakech
TUNISIA
Tripoli
Misratah
Benghazi
Alexandria
Cairo
EGYPT
Asyut
Sohag
Aswan
ALGERIA
LIBYA
WESTERN SAHARA
MAURITANIA
Nouakchott
MALI
NIGER
CHAD
Lake Chad
Abeche
N'Djamena
SUDAN
Port Sudan
Atbara
Khartoum
Wad Medani
El Obeid
Kosti
ERITREA
Asmara
DJIBOUTI
Djibouti
SOMALIA
Addis Ababa
ETHIOPIA
Dakar
SENEGAL
Banjul
Bissau
GUINEA
Bamako
Bobo Dioulasso
BURKINA FASO
Niamey
Ouagadougou
BENIN
NIGERIA
Abuja
Parakou
Korhogo
Sokode
COTE D'IVOIRE
GHANA
Yamoussoukro
Porto-Novo
Monrovia
LIBERIA
SIERRA LEONE
Abidjan
Accra
Lome
TOGO
Moundou
Sarh
CENTRAL AFRICAN REPUBLIC
CAMEROON
Bangui
Malabo
Yaounde
EQUATORIAL GUINEA
GABON
Libreville
REP. OF THE CONGO
Kisangani
DEMOCRATIC REPUBLIC OF THE CONGO
Nimule
UGANDA
Kampala
KENYA
Merca
Mogadishu
Lake Victoria
Nairobi
Kigali
RWANDA
BURUNDI
Bujumbura
Arusha
Tanga
Zanzibar
Dar es Salaam
Dodoma
TANZANIA
Tchibanga
Brazzaville
Kinshasa
Pointe-Noire
Mbuji-Mayi
Atlantic Ocean
Indian Ocean
Luanda
ANGOLA
Lobito
Huambo
Lubumbashi
Ndola
MALAWI
ZAMBIA
Lilongwe
Salima
Lusaka
Blantyre
MOZAMBIQUE
COMOROS
Mahajanga
Toamasina
Antananarivo
MADAGASCAR
Reunion (France)
Harare
ZIMBABWE
Bulawayo
Gweru
Beira
NAMIBIA
BOTSWANA
Windhoek
Gaborone
Pietersburg
Pretoria
Mmabatho
Mbabane
Maputo
SWAZILAND
Maseru
LESOTHO
Kimberley
Bloemfontein
Durban
SOUTH AFRICA
Umtata
East London
Cape Town
Port Elizabeth

Nairobi: Kenyan 3 million inhabitant capital. Instead of signing off their reports with this background western journalists prefer to show Africas poor and their Ghetos.

Mombasa Kenyas Beach resort at the Indian Ocean. The city is haven and a meeting point for Safari partner „hunters“.

AUTHORS NOTE

Safari "Partner" is a true story of my life and of others caught up in mixed and transcontinental-"love"-relationships. It is not only a biography of the characters involved, but also an intellectual analysis and critical view of the surrounding factors that lead to these relationships Factors like gender inequality, sexual exploitation, poverty, global politics, social stratification, Germanys integration politics, racism, economic marginalization and neo-colonialism. The Safari Partner characters are real; I have only changed their names for personal privacy. For the sake of fairness I have to state here that all the characters in the book do not represent all the mixed marriages in Germany but they do represent the majority of the lot. So join me in the Safari to what poor world citizens perceive to be the Promised Land, Western Europe, and reel in the wheel of hope, fortune, expectations and disappointments. Safari Njema! Fare thee well! Gute Reise!

DEDICATION

To my grandmother

I understand when one travels through the winds of life, strength and experience is gained, both positive and negative. I dedicate this book to my mentor, by beloved grandmother Musaili. Born in the early 1916, she defied century old customs. As a teenage girl she refused arranged marriage to an eighty year old man, fled a distance of two hundred kilometres on foot through the wilderness, from Nzaui to Masii, through the forests of Masimba, then heavily inhabited by lions, married a young man of her choice, got an only daughter and stood by her even when the people around her never saw a daughter as a child, retained her culture and religion though Christian neighbours claimed the peppermint leaves she was using for curative reasons and which Africans had for centuries used to cure cold and flu patients were satanic, yet they bought and used European packaged peppermints terming it as civilised and modern! She danced and maintained "Kilumi-dance" to this day when the said dance was labelled as devilish, wore African ornaments and clothes, yet the converted Christian neighbours named them as satanic. She withstood all sorts of cultural discrimination. To her and the nomadic Maasai people of East Africa, I salute.

ACKNOWLEGEMENTS

I would like to thank the following people for being part of my life in the world of "Safari Partner"

To Jacinta, Mwikali, Mbula, Roger, Peter Nzioka and Paul, your loyalty to friendship is legendary.

To Rainer and Ingrid, thanks for reminding me of the fragility of life.

To the Cool boys from Friedenau: Patrick Christ, Mesut, Norman Stahl, Antony, Raphael, Dennis and Xin-Ling, thank you for welcoming Matata and making his life easy in his new start in Berlin.

To Rolf W. they say that the longest Journey in life begins with a single step, ours has just began!

To Frank Wischman, Tillman Römer, Uwe Schiller, Heidi, Marion, Christian Stahl and Susan Gabler, thank you all for being my the family I loath and love in Germany.

To Nthenya Musau and your son Francis, thank you for opening for me the secret world of Mzungus and their Safari Partners, from Malindi, Kenya to Berlin it has been a world of experience. My tears go to you and your little son for the violence and trauma you experienced in Germany.

To Kira Dahmann thanks, you were not only the "Safari partner" translator but a real companion!

Last but not least thanks to my family and everyone who knows me and might not understand my reasons for writing this book: No hard feelings, the truth had to be told. Courage overcame all self-imposed censorship!

PROLOGUE

It has been exactly Eleven years since I came to Germany. Eleven good years, years of good and bad experiences, years of unpredictable and unimaginable experiences. Maybe it is destiny, but sometimes destiny can be sweet and sour. I have written this book with a very strong personal and humanitarian gesture. In a way I want to help future victims of the life I experienced, in the least I can, and if possible, equip them with the information and courage one needs in such situations. I must thank my upbringing and God (Ngai Mumbi, Yahweh or Allah, whatever you perceive God to be) for giving me the courage to go through what I did without breaking down. You will agree with me that some people having lived the kind of life I led in Kenya, and having to go through what I did in Germany would either commit suicide or end up in psychiatric centres. I also wish to thank my son Matata for the support and strength he gave me and always does; I am sure without him I would not have had the energy to go on. Those people who have children know that a child imparts a special energy in a parent, really mystic in a way, and puts hopes in hopeless situations. It is really a gift! Lastly but not the least I must state here that the characters in this book are real, people I came across in Germany, I have only changed their names for personal privacy, their experiences are not fiction but reality.

I gave my book the title "Safari Partner" because of its different meanings. Safari is a Kiswahili word, the East African Lingua Franca, estimated to be spoken by over 50 million people in Kenya, Uganda, Tanzania, Somalia, Congo, Rwanda and Djibouti. Safari means a sojourner or traveller. Among the 42 Kenyan languages the name is also similar to Msafari, Kyalo, Mutembei etc. A person who travels to far away destinations is called Msafiri. When children in East Africa have such a name, it means that they were born when their parents were travelling in a far away region, hence the act of "SAFIRI" to make a SA-

FARI. Kenya's rich tourism industry, from the days of Hemingway to date, popularized the word Safari worldwide.

The characters in my book met their "partners" while on safari, hence the safari partner. I have put the word Partner in italics for I don't see these relationships as partnership in the real sense of the word. In a normal partnership people share, there is a balance, equilibrium and best wishes in almost all undertakings. Unfortunately my experience with "Safari partners" in Germany was quite the opposite! I can only sum up these unions as opportunistic. The main female partners in my book are Kenyans, Kenya being the only African country in Germany-with more women than men. This is not by chance. Unlike North and West Africa, whose citizens come to Germany to study or are married to their countrymen, the majority of female Kenyans in Germany are the wives of German men and Kenya's successful tourism industry plays a major role in this. In this narration Tara tells her story and I narrate the story of Bernd und Gina. Last but not least I wish to state here that this book is not intended to hurt anyone, but instead wants to be an eye opener for those who seek knowledge including past, present and future victims of "Safari Partner!"

TARA'S STORY

To tell you the truth, I really don't know where to begin. Not because I do not know what to narrate, but because there is so much to tell, so much has happened to me since I boarded a Lufthansa Airbus on an April night in 1997 at the Kenyatta International Airport in Nairobi, Kenya.
It was a tearful night, a night as fate would have it, as it has always been full of coincidences. This was the night I coincidentally met my ex-friend Kitüsya on the same flight. Kitüsya was and still is a prominent Kenyan businessman and politician and he was part of the reason why I left Kenya, call it coward-

ice, but our turbulent relationship was enough reason to make one look for escape, but that is another story! It was like the past meeting the present, it was a symbol of the hopelessness and uncertainty of the journey I was now embarking on.

On this particular night I was mourning, mourning for leaving my beloved country Kenya, mourning for not knowing when to to return, mourning for leaving my cherished journalism career, mourning for leaving my family behind, friends too. And really mourning for my life and my son's uncertain future. I was leaving Kenya for Germany with only one aim, to secure a better future for my son Matata.

Matata was born in Kenya, just like the popular tourist word. In Kiswahili language the word means trouble or problems. Maybe you have heard the popular Kenyan saying "Kenya Hakuna Matata", now adapted by the children's film, Lion King. Locally the saying only means that Kenya is peaceful, taking into consideration that most of our neighbours are at war or experience political turmoil. Kenya borders the war-torn Somalia, Ruanda is not far and Idi Amin was once our neighbour and don't forget Sudan and the conflict between Eritrea and Ethiopia. No wonder in 1989 a one orally talented Kenyan education minister, no other than Oloo Aringo, called Kenya an island of peace at our graduation ceremony at Nairobi University. I simply named my son Matata because from the day I conceived him I knew I had looked for trouble. Don't misunderstand me, I love my son more than myself, but the decision I took because of him thrushed me into a world I had never imagined. We have a saying in my tribe that the moment you become a parent you worry until death. It is the love that makes us worry, though hard to understand for most children especially if they are grown-ups and Mama is still "mothering" them! The Akamba tribe, which I belong to, is one of 42 tribes in Kenya and names are given according to events, seasons and ancestors. If you bear a child in the forest collecting firewood, that child is called Bush, children born at night are called Mutuku or, if a girl, Nduku.

Matata is an offspring of Kenyan and German parentage. I met his father on an official trip in 1992 in Berlin. What started as an adventure – romantic Spree – resulted in a child a year later! Call it the beginning of Matata or naivety, but to this day I see it as destiny.

I met Karl-Heinz in one summer afternoon in the Kreuzberg district of Berlin. I had come to this popular multicultural district by chance. I was in Berlin on a seminar organised by the Kenya Union of Journalists (KUJ) and the then International Institute of Journalism Berlin (IIJB). On this particular day, contrarily to what our lecturer, one Frau Schulz, had said, I decided to board a train alone and see the city of Berlin. She had cautioned us about travelling alone, more so in the Eastern part, the former Eastern sections of the city. After the fall of the famous Berlin Wall in 1989 the Eastern part was said to be frequented by "skinheads". These are jobless youths who believe their social and financial handicaps are a result of immigrants to Germany. These youths proclaimed themselves as victims of the German unification and relaxed immigration policies. Recently a German politician in Brandenburg found himself in trouble with his political mates when he accepted the problem and even advised dark-skinned people not to venture in some parts of former East Germany lest they risked their lives. It was unfortunate for him that he said the correct words at the wrong time. Considering the German Nazi-history and then the country preparing to hold the football World Cup, his remarks were not politically or should I say patriotically correct. The truth is that foreigners in Germany are daily confronted with racism, more so if you have a black skin. It does not have to be the recent brutal attack on Indians in Mugeln and also on an Ethiopian-German in Potsdam. I think ordinary Germans should accept that there is a problem. You see it in public transport when white German passengers avoid to share and squeeze themselves in chairs, leaving a whole empty bench to a non-white. This summer I boarded a bus from Zehlendorf to Friedenau (M48) Unique in what is claimed to be a multicultural

Germany capital was that the bus was being driven by a blackman. In the course of the drive, in entered to construction workers in their tainted aprons and remarked loudly,"A blackman as a driver, I will be grateful when I get out of the bus alive!" Such attitude did not amaze me, I have lived long enough in Germany to hear them but what amazed me was that not a single passenger rebuked the two.Daily black children are bullied in schools and called "Niggers". I was actually shocked when I asked my son about it, then in elementary school, and he thought there was nothing wrong about his classmate Anthony being called "nigger" in school. My son's black classmate is a German of Ghanaian descent. To my son this was a daily happening and normal.

To cut a long story short, it was dangerous for a foreigner to travel in the Eastern part of Berlin. Many foreigners have lost their lives in the hands of skinheads; Africans are more vulnerable because of their distinguished skin color! Some skinheads go as far as throwing foreigners from moving speedy trains.
With all this in mind I took the risk of travelling alone, but I guess that is part of my character, wild, daring or naïve, whichever way you see it!
On this humid summer afternoon I got off at the station Schlesisches Tor and there was a reason for this. My eyes were attracted by a crowded Second-Hand-market and I decided to look at the wares.
I took a walk around the market and to my surprise I heard somebody shout my name, my full name! Unbelievable. I checked the direction of the voice and to my surprise I saw a crowd of about ten African men! Unbelievable! Who could know me in Berlin! If it was in Nairobi it would not be a surprise, but Berlin of all places! The only person who knew my name in Berlin was a Kenyan photo journalist, one Yusuf W, a photo journalist whom I had left behind at the institute. So for me this was puzzling.

It was even more puzzling because the men who were smiling and heading towards me were all unfamiliar. And if my African judgement was to go by, they all looked like west Africans. I must mention here that it is easy for a person from Africa to distinguish the origin of Africans. West Africans are muscular built, with a wide mouth and big flat noses, whereas most east Africans are part from what we call western Bantus. They are tall, slender, with long sharp noses. In Germany a Roberto Blanco-look is a West African (Ghana Nigeria etc) look while "Dieters Nadel" is a classical East African (Kenya, Sudan Ethiopia, etc) look. What is actually known as Afro-Americans is mostly a west African population. Their physical features are very distinct from Brazilian Blacks who came mainly from Angola. By the way, talk of lost "patents", the Samba music in Brazil has its origin in Angola but not in Spain or Portugal. Or do the former Spaniards in Argentina have anything similar?

Back to my fellow Africans! We were all excited as it is the custom in a foreign country, for we felt like a family. The man who actually shouted my name was a Kenyan working with the foreign ministry in Nairobi but who was attending a seminar in Berlin. Apart from seeing me on television back home, he was once a college-mate at Nairobi University. As if to prove my assessment, the rest of the group were from Ghana and Nigeria. As I came to learn later they frequented such markets to buy cheap clothes for their extended families in Africa. To my surprise one of the Ghanaians shouted: "Hey, sister, are you married? I want to marry you." Instead of shock I only laughed, it was not normal for a stranger to address me that way but, as it would turn out, the man was only exercising his male chauvinistic charm! I also came to learn that West African people, who are actually the majority of Africans living abroad, refer to each other as "sister and brother" as a sign of brotherhood and solidarity. So in this case a sister did not mean blood relationship as we see it in Kenya. He insisted on talking to me and invited me to his apartment. Such an approach was initially like a joke, however we exchanged telephone numbers and I promised to visit him.

Our visit took some time to materialise, for the IIJB group had to travel to visit important Berlin sites and also the Eastern city of Dresden for a two week excursion. In Berlin we toured its famous river Spree on beautiful boats. The tour saw us go round the 3 million German metropolis. For the African journalists it was an emotional tour to visit the spot and see the conference room where the partition of Africa, our continent, had been done. Our trip also saw us visit the remaining part of famous Berlin wall. We visited the city border control formerly dividing east and west Berlin, the famous Checkpoint Charlie. At the said control point, hawk-eyed Americans used to guard west Berlin face to face with East German boarder security. I understand that on this spot one could really sense the tension of the cold war and its fragility. Today it is almost impossible to imagine that one's passport was stamped when visiting another part of the city. Politics! But that was the reality then, a divided Germany. Our city tour saw us visit the Brandenburg Gate where once Napoleon marched his troops and the famous Sanssouci Castle. Using a small boat on the Teltow Canal in the Berlin environs, we saw the house were the Americans made the decision to bomb Hiroshima and Nagasaki, and last but not least we were shown the bunker where Hitler spent his last moments.
The city of Berlin is rich of both positive and negative history. Then we travelled with a luxury bus to the city of Dresden. I say luxury, for 1992 few developing countries could boast of having a modern bus with a cockpit resembling an airbus. The bus was also equipped with a toilet. The modern road network looked like a dream, technology and beauty merging in romance. I imagined the contrast of this development with the many potholes in Kenyan roads.
Along the route to Dresden, we saw a lonely castle in the woods with a tragic love story. Our tour guide said that one of

the German kings once deported his mistress there to avoid family conflicts. Unknowingly, the mistress believed that the king would continue his escapades with her but waited until death without ever seeing him again. Rumour has it to this day that villagers neighbouring the castle still see the ghost of the sad and lonely woman at night. I imagined the times and the mistress living in an isolated woodland and then the only mode of transport was horses.

The city of Dresden turned out to be a worthwhile trip. Museums filled with historical paintings and royal jewellery, the then renowned church (Frauenkirche) destroyed during the Second World War and now restored, the river Elbe among many wonderful sites.

When we came back, however, true to his word Kofi, the man from Ghana, called me. We arranged a visit and since he promised to cook Ghanaian food for me, I decided to take two of my girl friends. They were radio journalists, Penzi from Radio Tanzania and Helen from Sierra Leone. To be sincere, we were all excited to meet Africans who had lived in this metropolitan city longer than us. On one Saturday afternoon we arrived at Kofi's one-room flat in Stresemannstraße, Kreuzberg, district of Berlin.

To tell you the truth, my first observation was shock. In this small room there were more than ten black men and God knows, the high sound of music that was being played, really everybody was talking at the top of their voices and I would call it a miracle that people could still communicate in such an atmosphere.

I thanked myself for having brought my friends, for I could not imagine coming to such a place to meet strangers alone. Not because I was scared, but I kept reminding myself that one could never be sure with strangers. In this small room there was only one bed and if you could not secure a place to sit, then you had to stand. Kofi and his "brothers" welcomed us warmly but before I could sit down, he summoned me to his small balcony. Observation number one: This was strange. As African customs

demand, I expected him to offer me a seat, though there was not any, and a drink. Unfortunately or fortunately this was not the case.
Kofi did not waste his time revisited his proposal. He was also armed with what he perceived to be his important weapon-in-hand, a maroon German passport! For me really this was strange, this was a man, a stranger to me, directly wanting to marry me! Kofi did not know who I was, and my basic upbringing told me that I should know the background of a future partner and worse still, there were no feelings between us.
I found his proposal ridiculous, chauvinistic and, to be sincere, absurd. Worse still, he kept on emphasising that he had "papers" and showed me his German passport.
In all fairness as a Kenyan, this was ridiculous. Now that I have lived in Germany for years I understand this mentality, but to be sincere, then, all he was telling me was meaningless. I wish you saw his eyes when he told me about his German nationality, laughable, I would say!
To Kofi's shock I asked him why he had relinquished his Ghanaian citizenship. The answer I got was only a question: "Don't you know how many black girls would jump to such an offer?"

Unfortunately for Kofi I never jumped to his generous offer, in his opinion a privilege, a privilege to marry an African with German citizenship. This for Kofi meant, as I later came to learn, getting papers without having to labour and pay, being able to work in Germany and more, having a strong African man to sexually satisfy you. As I later came to learn if a foreigner married a German, one had to be a "slave" for three years before one could get their "papers". To many who had gone through this process, "hell period", as it was called, was not an easy task. According to some of the victims I talked to, it was like working in what we call in Kenya the "hardship zone". These are remote semi-desert regions where Kenya borders with Somalia and Sudan, it seldoms rains there, they are sparsely populated and meteorologically cruel. Kenyans working in such remote areas receive incentives in order to boost their working morale. Most mixed marriages in Germany could be equated to the Kenyan hardship zone services, the only difference being that there are no incentives! In this hard period you have to satisfy a German's sexual needs and if you are a woman, clean his house, services he could not get from a German woman. In a normal German household both partners share domestic responsibilities equally, but not the majority of Germans married to foreigners. I must state here that in the word foreigner I mostly emphasise partners from Africa, Latin America, eastern Europe and Asia. A case is told of a black girl who boldly told her German husband that she was not a "Putzfrau" (which means cleaning woman). To her dismay he answered: "Negro, if I wanted a wife and not a cleaning woman, I would have married a German woman." The African men on their case "were dying an slow ego-death". In my observation, most African men married to German women are ordinary citizens from low income groups in villages and beach towns in Africa. When I talk of villagers I mean villagers! Don't compare the German rural area with an African village, some of these Africans have never lived in a house with flowing water or electricity in their home county. They come from real rural areas in Africa, have never used electricity or flowing water, the male authority is next to God and women are there to be seen but not to be heard! Such men come from poor families and have very basic or no education and no official job in their own countries. With regard to this background, such men and women have no chance in their countries, no jobs and tend to end up in Germany where they can still earn a living. They come to Germany either by marriage or as registered political refugees. Mention it, from the Kurdish population in Turkey to the beaches of Thailand, from the famous Nigerian market of Kano to the port of Takoradi in Ghana, from the white sandy beaches of Mombasa and Malindi in Kenya to Maasai Mara the aim was one, destination Germany, the land of Mercedes and Siemens!

Due to historical and colonial reasons, Germany has a special group of foreigners when compared to Britain, France or the U.S.A. Also due to historical reasons, foreigners who went to such countries were well integrated and language plays a major role in this. Ironically to note that the Partition of Africa was done in Berlin, yet Germany as a country had very little to do with the majority of African countries. Africans, who were better off, went to former colonial masters, studied, and went back to Africa, and those who remained were absorbed in the normal systems of the countries involved. Such Africans like Jomo Kenyatta of Kenya, Kwame Nkruma from Ghana or even the late self- proclaimed President for life, Kamuzu Banda from Malawi, ended up being the ruling elite in independent Africa. The European citizens of the countries in question also learned to live with foreigners, shared ideas as students and accepted them too in the workforce in the white color jobs. This process played a major role in attitude and integration. Germany on the other hand accepted the first foreign workers from Turkey during the economic boom after the Second World War as what is referred to as "guest workers". This first generation of Turkish immigrants, mostly Kurds, set what is normally seen as "foreign workers jobs" in Germany, namely manual jobs like house workers, factory workers and any dirty job that Germans considered inferior. For generations this set a trend and many ordinary Germans to this day still believe that foreigners have nothing to offer in their elite job cadre. Not because they are racists but because of the historical background, the Turks were followed by north African guest workers, then the Angolans and Mozambicans to former East Germany. Unlike Britain, Germany has never seen a black man in its parliament and believes me, such an attitude plays a major role in integration. Unlike America, where one is given the hope of a limitless future and success, the initial immigrants in Germany were given the tag "guest workers", indirectly portraying their impermanent stay in the country. Such a title says more than words. Don't be surprised that then the Kurds, who were the guest workers in

Germany, built their cocoons, for they felt unwanted, used and segregated. Unlike in France, Britain and the U.S.A, where immigrants felt that if they worked hard, they had a chance of integration, in Germany one was made aware that one was here to work and leave just like a machine that has outlived its use. Most of the initial guest workers never bothered to learn the German language and instead passed on their language and traditions to their offspring hoping to return home one day. This kind of official segregation in my opinion made the Turkish immigrants feel segregated.

Years down the lane, the German politicians, instead of accepting that they made a mistake, turned against the second generation of these "guest workers" and blamed them for being closed and difficult to integrate. The German citizens too listened to their politicians who made them feel secure by declaring the Turkish immigrants as guests. So don't be surprised if you arrive in Germany and the first question you receive goes like this "Hallo, where do you come from? How long are you staying? When are you going back?" Reminds me of a Catholic litany in a catechism school. Every foreigner who is in Germany has been asked this question. It is surprising for me that the way these questions are asked sound like a rehearsal and I used to wonder how a country's citizens could have learned such preformulated questions? As an African I was sensitive to this kind of formulation, for where I come from, a guest is treated like a king for that is believed to bring luck and wisdom for me. This kind of "interrogation" was impolite and made me feel unwanted. In the last lower house elections, a politician of Turkish descent was admitted to hospital after an attack from a Neo-Nazi who still could not come to terms with the idea of an immigrant offspring politician in the German parliament. Yet in neighbouring France Nicholas Sarkozy, a child of an immigrant, has been elected prime minister. In the USA too, Barack Obama, a child of a Kenyan Havard Guest student and Awhite American mother from Hawaii has now has now won the presidential election with a landslide to become the first coloured

American President. His victory was acclaimed worlwide with Kenya his fathers homeland declaring a national holiday. Though good intented the Kenyan government should have used the occassion to firmly implement its consitution and make it mandatory for Kenyan men to pay child support. Remember Baracks father left him at a tender age and without the effort of his mother and grandparents in America, Kenya would not had the chance to celebrate in Obamas success!They say he has the charisma of J.F. Kennedy. On the other hand the majority of German media was more interested on Obamas colour than his intellect and charisma. I found this very narrow minded and to some extend annoying

Just like word spreads around, the strength of the German economy saw the coming of Africans too, the availability of unskilled labour in Germany. They too came, Africans with no or little education, Germany needed such a workforce, but unlike the early Turkish immigrants they had to meet strict immigration regulations. These were Africans who had no future in their countries. Either their parents were too poor to educate them or they were Africans who wanted to escape low paid manual jobs in their countries. Many immigrants to date tend to migrate to Germany to avoid economic hardships and strict border controls from countries like Britain and France who have experience with migrants from their former colonies. Financially capable Africans who want to send their children abroad for further studies send them to former colonial masters and language plays a major role in this.

To date the Ghanaian community is the largest African immigrant group in Germany. It is a mixture of ordinary and educated Africans. Official figures as of 1999 show that Ghanaians living in Germany totalled to 22,602 out of which 12,889 were male and 9,713 were female. The number is bound to be higher, taking into consideration that the west African immigrants tend to prefer western passports for certain reasons. An intellectual immigrant from Cameroon or Nigeria has better chances of looking for a white color job in countries like France or England if he holds a European passport.

Unlike East Africa, mainly Kenya, West Africa has a big group of educated Africans. Those who studied in Europe have no problems with the language and end up in the job market. Career opportunities for African intellectuals are poor due to language and restrictive citizenship laws. One would be excused to think that the German laws were passed with the notion that immigrants have no business in Germany's skilled workforce. For years it has been very difficult for African academic immigrants to integrate. The biggest hurdle has always been the language and initial government language courses seemed to favour the stereotype German immigrants, manual workers. The courses were very basic and cut off say a journalist who needed an intensive course to practise his profession. Fortunately the Immigration Office seems to wake up from this limbo and is now offering an intensive language course as part of the integration efforts. Whereas the USA capitalises and utilises foreign academics, luring them into migrating to the US to this date, leading to what has come to be known as "Brain drain".

Educated foreigners have been locked out for a long time in the German white color jobs. I believe it is for the countries integration benefit to have an active and productive immigrant population rather than the classic "social welfare benefit foreign parasite". A well integrated foreigner with a future in Germany has a stable and productive family rather than an alienated, jobless, immigrant whose children do not also have a conducive family unit. It leads to crime, bitterness and a vicious circle of poverty. It works against the country. The US, for example, has a booming call centre industry owing to its diversion of telephone services to the cheap labour market in India. If one needs services in America, one phones and the answer is given to you in English by somebody in New Delhi. In Germany there are enough immigrants who could offer such services, but instead the German companies in question lock out foreigners in their adverts when they underline in capital letters

“we are looking for native English speakers”, tell me how many English natives are in Germany? Foreigners from Commonwealth countries with good education speak the language perfectly. Or do all native Germans speak perfect German? I think when we talk of integration in this country we should also talk of Germany’s global integration to understand each other. It can’t work on one way highway!
It is this “integration alienation policy” that has led some educated Africans, mainly not by choice, far away from their learned professions into private businesses like shipping and what is commonly known as “Afro shops”. Interesting to note too is that Kenya unlike all the other African citizens in Germany has the highest female population. According to Federal Office of Statistics, in 2002 there were 4,431 Kenyans, out of which 1568 were male and 2,863 were female. Reasons behind this is that unlike West African immigrants who are mainly refugees and students, most Kenyan immigrants are “Safari partners”. This arrival pattern is also changing, for the Safari partners, who are mainly from socially disadvantaged groups, have now managed with their “improved economic” status to educate their relatives back home and we are now seeing young generations of Kenyans with relatives in Germany who are now enrolling at German universities. Some Kenyan au-Pairs are also enrolling at German universities. Then unlike today Germany did not give Green Cards and in any case, such Africans did not fit the category of foreign workers who are employed in the IT sector, so the easiest way out was to marry a German citizen to get a work permit. The strict immigration policies though, meant to protect German citizens ended up making them victims. Unscrupulous immigrants from Asia, eastern Europe and West Africa, mainly Ghana and Nigeria, flocked Germany and married its citizens, sired children and abandoned them after they got their resident visa. With the post-war booming economy, Germans travelled on holiday worldwide. Among their favourite destination is Kenya and the country to date gets millions of tourists annually. These visits too set the trend of

Beach girls and boys marrying German tourists. Many Germans who marry such Africans are usually not equipped with the understanding of cross-cultural relationships. The majority of such Germans are ordinary citizens with a lot of social shortcomings ranging from machoism, lack of self-esteem, alcoholism, idleness, joblessness, lack of personal hygiene, school-dropouts, obesity etc. And let alone understand such a cross range of cultural diversities, such Germans have also a hard time in their own society, they are either discriminated against because of their anti-social behaviours, say like alcoholism or too old for a partner in Germany or obesity. The western society lays great importance on weight loss, backed by television adverts on all sorts of products, from food to lifestyle and success. Germans with social shortcomings tend to look for partners in poor third-world countries. Interesting to observe too is the kind of German women married to African men, the majority are twenty or so years older than their husbands. The majority of them don't work or are too fat with 3-4 children from different partners. In fact, these kind of marriages has tended to create the image that African men love fat women, yes, a lot of societies in Africa appreciate a fat and proportional woman of the same age with a man, but not a 200 kilograms-50- ear-old woman with an athletic 20- year- old African man! The African men back home are even proud to say and I quote: "A skinny woman does not have shock absorbers for African tools, a real African man has the tools for a big woman!" Most mixed marriages in Germany are doomed and end after the attainment of the resident visa and believe me, such women never get the opportunity to ever see the families of their young husbands, for the young men are ashamed of such unions. Exceptions are there, too. Good German men and women who think universally, love universally but unfortunately choose to listen to their heart and body but not to logic! They marry beautiful and handsome foreigners without taking into consideration the basic foundations of a relationship like common interests. Good German men who get into quarrels with their wives for wanting to share domestic chores. Some of these women come from patriarchal societies where it is an offence for a man to wash dishes! She loses her mind for seeing a man working in the kitchen and she is even sad for thinking that she married a lesser man! Take an example of a German intellectual who travels to Kenya on a Safari, sees a beautiful Maasai girl, marries her and brings her to Germany, expects her to wear high-heeled shoes for the first time, designer clothes and go to concerts and appreciate Mozart! Or how about a German architect who travels to Brazil, meets a girl in a bar whose only job and pastime is to commercially wait for the tourists while drinking, she has never known another life and when he brings her to Germany he expects her to undergo a "metamorphosis". He wonders why she keeps on drinking and spending her afternoons in bars. He actually wonders why she cannot keep time when she has an appointment! He even thinks she is ungrateful after he "rescued" her from a ghetto and put her in his nice apartment in Berlin-Steglitz! What he fails to understand is that what she needs is counselling and integration more than his golden credits cards which she uses unsparingly! Talk of the impossible! Human beings are not liquids to be assimilated and dissolved, my dear fellows! And you know, what amazes me is the shock they get for not understanding why these "foreigners" are not grateful for being accepted in such big civilizations and their fruits of freedom! I am sometimes at a loss when I meet such Germans who even see themselves as victims, for they all along believed they were in real relationships. A good friend of mine, Siggi, once travelled to Kenya and fell in love with a 20- year-old callgirl. Mind you, he is 62 years old, has undergone two heart operations and he is jobless! I told him point blank that he was making a mistake! You should have seen him yelling at me and telling me to stop discouraging him. He said the girl lived in a ghetto in Nairobi and he even shared her carton house with no running water and she was caring and loving. Before he brought her to Berlin, he proudly showed her photo to any African he came across. They just smiled, the story was all too

familiar. I just knew that the old man was infatuated. I gave up. The same advice he was given by the clerks at the marriage office in Berlin, they received the same reaction. They too had seen the fate of many such unions. He later married this girl and the moment she received her three year visa she never smiled nor shared his bed! He received my shoulder to cry on and apologised for not listening.
I was not surprised by Siggis behaviour. It is an old story for Safari partners. Personally I would not call them so, for such unions are based on opportunism. In a partnership people share many things they have in common, but not in this kind of relationships. Both characters are opportunists and use the union as a scapegoat in order to draw off the attention from their own problems. What surprised me more were my friends bitter remarks and insults of Africans in general and believe me, he knows many in Berlin. He labelled them "ungrateful bastards", I could not believe it. He never saw any wrongdoing in his marriage. He saw the girl he picked from a Nairobi slum as ungrateful. I could not take it. I frankly told him that if he found the 20- year-old Kenyan girl ungrateful why not marry a 20-year-old German girl? He never answered but instead smiled at me sardonically. I think my point hit home. He realised that what he did with a poor third world citizen was not possible in his home yard. He knew very well that such behaviours were not accepted in Germany among normal folk. It was an exclusive domain of millionaires and playboys and somehow the society tolerated that. But not the likes of my dear friend Siggi! Call it living in a lie! Unfortunately such relationships are for conveniences, a lonely socially rejected German with a desperate poor immigrant looking for residence and better life in Europe! Believe me they never work! And what is even amusing is that those involved don't seem to understand why? They just keep on accusing each other for not being grateful! The foreigners too are under time pressure to acquire documents to guarantee their stay in Germany. Apart from their exotic wonderful sexual performance, they have nothing in common with

their spouses. Most of these men have had no formal education in their countries, no official job and the only role they saw a woman play in their village is that of wife and mother. Not surprising when they marry German women here they expect the same and believe me, such relationships never work. A German woman with a basic education also knows her rights as a citizen, she grew up in families where the father shared domestic work with his wife, and now in 2007 she marries a man who beats her and cannot even take his plate back to the kitchen after eating food she has bought, talk of impossible relationships! Weekends here are family days, some of these Africans grew up knowing that men don't change nappies, cook or even stay home on weekends with their wives. Germans married to Kenyan men, don't be surprised if you visit your African in-laws and the young men of the family sit like kings while expecting their old and frail Mama to cook for them! Such men don't enter the kitchen, old however the mother is, she is still to them a woman, and a woman's place is the kitchen, a very inferior corner for a MAN! There are still families in Kenya where the appearance of a man sends chills in a women's or family gathering, actually it is not a rare occurrence in my tribe to see children back off from their conversations when their father arrives. Such families are administered by fear rather than respect and the coming home of the male household sends chill in the family. It is not unusual to see a man announce his presence not by greeting, but by a sound like clearing his throat, to ordinary Kenyans this only means the lion, Simba, has arrived! Children scurry and clear the way by going to their quarters and the wife dutifully and softly brings the man his meal, whether he eats it or not will be his decision, he can leave it untouched but the wife will not dare ask why he is not partaking the meal, sounds archaic but a reality in Kenya where I come from. Surprisingly this kind of fear makes the men feel proud, to them it is a sign of respect!

Here in Germany both partners take the children out, cook and spend time together and if not, one has an explanation where he is going, of course somewhere where the wife can reach him on telephone! I'm sure some Kenyan men must be laughing themselves to death when they read this. They might even say "these are no men" It is said that habit is second to nature, so such men when they come here, they want to treat the German women the same and believe me, they have no chance! Some married men in Kenya are used to going to bars on Fridays with their mistresses and come home on Monday to change their clothes, their marital obligation does not go beyond paying house rent and siring children whom they rarely see. On the other hand their German wives waste no time and effort to westernise African spouses and believe me, this in a lot of occasions ends up in conflicts. The German husbands have their share of problems, too. The majority of German men married to foreigners did so because they have a problem getting a partner at home. Such problems range from low self-esteem, machoism, weight problems to hygiene, finance or even adventure. By marrying a foreigner, such men try to run away from their social shortcomings in Germany, just like the way an ostrich buries it head in the sand. Such men assume that by marrying a foreigner from a poor country, they would get the upper hand of the situation, but believe me, its wishful thinking. Due to their low self esteem they avoid equal thinking partners in Germany and look for wives like dolls in third world countries to boost their low self esteem. They avoid independent thinkers, for these challenge their male authority or machoism that has no place in developed countries. They do not look for partners but sexual dolls and free house helps. Any woman, black or white, will not live because of poverty forever with a man who cannot brush his teeth, a man who beats her, a man who weighs 200 kilograms and commands her like a brigadier or even a man who rarely takes a shower. I am not exaggerating! It happens here! If you want to prove this, why not take a walk to the next Asian shop in your district! You will see these two meter tall overweight German "grandpas" and a less than a meter 20-year-old Asian girl.

Have you ever asked yourself why it is rare in multicultural Berlin to see a black man walking side by side with his obese looking elderly white woman with colored children? It is rare. but what is common is a white woman pushing a pram with a colored child! It is not a coincidence! It has its reasons. On the other hand African men use metaphors to instil the doctrine of gender submissiveness, there is a saying that the man is the head and the woman the neck, so the neck follows the head! So a woman's role in a traditional African family where most of these men in Germany come from, is supportive, submissive, sacrificial without complaints and above all respect to the lion of the house. At no time does a traditional African woman shout at her man, let alone slap him! I guess foreigners from Africa or Asia will support me when I say the first thing a foreigner notices is when Germans shout, they shout not only at grown- ups, but at children too, and when you ask they say it is better than beating! For foreigners it is scaring and traumatising! I guess they think of it as a soft way of asserting authority! It is one of the many culture shocks that mixed couples are confronted with. Don't be surprised if an ordinary African woman tells you that she prefers to be beaten by her man than to be shouted at! In many communities today in Kenya there are a number of women who still believe that wife- beating is a sign of love! Old habits die hard! Many divorced African women in Germany tell me that they always jump when they hear a loud German male voice because of the memory of the shouts they experienced, call it trauma! So a "good African wife" does not shout at her "mighty" husband, not even when he brings his girlfriend home or sleeps out! Doing otherwise is unimaginable, so when a German woman shouts or engages in an argument with an African "warrior", it is the sure guarantee of the end of the relationship, of course he will persevere until he attains the residence visa! Really, to be fair you cannot blame these men, for they have not known another side of the coin. Like in Kenya where I come from, it is not a surprise to hear a mother of 15 daughters exclaim "I have no child, I only gave birth to daughters" when somebody asks her how many children she has. To such a woman a child is a son, and even the tone in which she answers depicts vividly her condemned destiny and position in society. A certain tribe in Western Kenya too is known to practise rituals which discriminate women from birth to death, and I mean it. When a daughter is born, the community and mostly women ululate once, but when a boy is born, they ululate twice or more to welcome the heir and backbone of the tribe, in death too, boys are buried in the family's fenced homestead, whereas a girl is buried outside the fence, for she is not considered as part of the family. A woman in many cultures in Africa is an outsider. In my village it is not a wonder when you knock at the door of a house and ask whether anybody is at home to get an answer from the women at home "There is nobody here, only I and the children". Such an answer from a mother to signal the absence of her husband only shows the nonentity of the position of women in my society. It is pathetic and institutionalized. A good number of African men living in Germany come from such backgrounds. Their great- grandmother behaved the same, so too do their mothers and their married sisters. So when you shout at an African man, you not only hurt his ego as a man to the core, but also challenge his position in society, unbelievable but a reality on our beautiful continent. Furthermore, in Africa's most tribes men undergo the rite of circumsion. This is not only a health practise due to our warm climate, but during this period men are separated from boys, women and girls to underscore their importance in society. The ritual states the important position of a man. It is performed surgery, accompanied with music and dance, festivities, and officially sealed with blessing by the leaders of the community who are men. It is hard to erase it from the minds of the people.

When it comes to the Afro-Euro marriages, children are the victims: by the time they grow up, the marriages are broken. So don't be surprised when you see a lot of colored children

brought up by single German mothers, the majority of these children too have never seen Africa with their eyes!
I one time worked for an organisation called Nachbarschaftsheim Schöneberg. They offer social services to families and I was sent to a family in Berlin Neukölln. What I saw and experienced there will linger in my memories for years. The first thing I realised was that the family way living in what is here referred to as a "social boiling point", indicated by the high-rise flats. Such massive high-rise housing would the famous writer Frantz Fanon today in Europe call "The Wretched of the Earth" residential quarters. I rang the bell and took a lift that brought me to a stinking 8th floor. So far, so good. Then suddenly a middle-aged woman opened the door to the flat! I was confronted with a pregnant German woman holding a one year old child and surrounding her were more than 5 colored children! Interesting to note was that the children were separated by one year age interval. Unconscious of the social stigma associated with such a family, the little children were all smiles and started introducing themselves to me in a chorus-like manner, of say solidarity. The manner in which they talked to me was in itself a search of identity and as an African I saw it as a way of trying to tell me "Hey, you are one of us". Like in a chorus, one after the other they introduced themselves, "my father comes from Ghana, mine is from Nigeria, mine is from Kongo, ours is from Mali", said two of the girls holding hands, "mine is from Senegal...", it went on and at last the pregnant mother in a too-knowing grown-up smile introduced herself as Tania and let me into the apartment. It was at that moment that I realised that none of the kids had said their name.
I was at a loss for words. I could not understand this woman's adventure with our black brothers, but you can be sure that I was looking forward to the story! The apartment was a mess, insects in the kitchen and stench. In the course of the day I too realised that all the six children and two grown-ups lived in this pathetic flat. Half an hour later a black man emerged from one of the bedrooms, in my opinion less than 25 years old. I later

learned from the 43-year-old Tania that the young man was a refugee from Nigeria and he was also the father of the toddler in hand and the current pregnancy. This was just the beginning, the man went into the kitchen, made himself breakfast and spent most of the day watching television and making phone calls from 7 different mobile phones which he displayed proudly on the table like precious possessions! You could hear his voice on phone from as far as the ground floor. Worse still, the children were kicking each other and asking for food while the young man was munching his food. I was beyond words. Part of my work in this family was to help with the housework and shop. While preparing breakfast, the young man, Bob, came to give me instructions on how to toast bread, according to him a very important procedure of getting rid of bacteria in the food. As if to emphasize the source of all these hygienic prescriptions, he even told me that he had studied biology at a University in Nigeria. I almost told him to go to hell! How could somebody living in such a filthy house talk of hygiene? I kept on subduing the rebel in me and continued cleaning!

I served the family breakfast and later had a talk with the lady of the house when the man left. I should also mention here that before he left, I had to intervene and separate the pregnant mother from Bob who she claimed was beating her and making her life hard. I just wondered how long I was going to last in this family. Later Tania narrated to me that she planned to change her locks that day to stop her friend visiting her from his refugee camp. She even boasted of knowing many key companies, for she often changed locks. Tania even never saw anything wrong in changing locks, for she claimed it was a common practise of many German women married to black men! She claimed they fought a lot lately because the African man was against the idea of her getting his second child. I was at a loss with words. These were two grown-ups who knew the usage of contraceptives. Worse still, this woman told me that she was a mother of eight. You cannot call that ignorance, something was very wrong with this lady but she never saw it that

way. She claimed she loved black men and planned to get sterilised (tubal ligation) and get no more babies.
In all her narrations she saw herself as the victim. She even showed me a photo of one of the fathers of her children whom she proudly said she deported to his poor country! To her this was punishment enough, or so she believed, like many of her country folk who marry foreigners. She thought the worst punishment for an African in Europe was to deport him. She was wrong. I later came to learn that the deported Ghanaian man, Ian, was happily working and living in the Netherlands. I could not resist asking her why she gave birth to children from so many different men. The answer was: "I was looking for happiness and landed in the wrong hands, mind you, I love black men and even after this pregnancy I am going to look for a new boyfriend in a Zairean disco near Alexanderplatz." Unfortunately, the innocent children in such relationships carry the bulk of the problems. Like in Tania's case, the bigger ones were already refusing to attend school and a social worker had to literally come and take one of the teenage boys to school. The fights with the mother's different boyfriends, the stress, the poverty and even lack of enough living space was no environment for a child to grow up. In my opinion, Tania was one of those Germans who unscrupulously and mercilessly used her children, social welfare and desperate African refugees for her own interests. She was a black sheep in her society and sought men who were in desperate situations. Such Germans are known to often say: "Ever since I met my foreign partner, I have no interest in German women (when a woman, German men), me and German women is history...". It is a self-made lie. The truth is, Germans like Tania are social misfits in Germany. With desperate foreigners they have it easy, period. Tania even claimed that the father of one of her children belonged to an aristocratic West African family. This too is a very commonly told story in Germany. The truth is, it is rare to find a royal member of a former British colony in Germany. Such families were privileged first to receive formal education and ended up being the

elite after the British left, and those residing outside Africa are either in France, England or the USA. So to imagine that the likes of Tania had partners from this group working as dishwashers in Germany is next to impossible. Not to mention that whoever they refer to as African royals have no education. It is one of the commonly told lies to the ignorant and uninformed paper marriage victims in Germany. It is cowardice and irresponsibility at its highest level.

With the government's social welfare for eight children, Tania had the means to get a bigger living space than the three rooms she had for 8 people. In my eyes it was an heinous crime against the children. After two weeks I could not take it any more and left. She screamed at the children like a military commander and in turn the children fought each other to express their frustration!

Safari partner children living in such ghettos have almost no chance in a normal social structure and careers. And just as all relationships go sour, bitterness follows, some German parents feed their children with a false image of Africa to discredit their runaway partners. With some of the parents the repression goes as far as even lying to their children that their fathers came from America and went back! (After the liberation of Germany from Hitler, allied forces from America, France, Britain and Russia remained behind to oversee a smooth transition) Surely some black Americans sired children here, but the majority came from West Africa! To be precise, Ghana and Nigeria. Interesting to note too was that many Africans also claimed to be Americans. I know this might sound disgusting to patriotic Africans in the Diaspora, but the African immigrants used this lie to avoid police controls, and by the time their Germans lovers realised this, they were already in love! A Nigerian friend of mine even told me that his countrymen purported to be Americans because that was what German women wanted to hear! One only wonders how the partners could not detect the strong west African accent in their English, a lot of cat-and-mouse-games in these relationships! African intellectuals are few in

Germany and the majority of Africans here lack the sense of pride of being an African, so don't be surprised if you meet Africans wearing T-shirts with American flag signs or even Jamaican ones, but speaking little or no English. Personally I have met Africans who claimed to come from Kuba but couldn't speak a single Spanish word! It is a combination of low self-esteem and lack of civil awareness... Africa has a lot to offer and those ordinary Germans, who have never been to Africa, and have an African neighbour with a radio can be forgiven when they think we should be so grateful to be in a country where we can eat, drink and listen to the radio at top volume! Or a common sight of an insensitive African man using a mobile phone, shouting at the top of his voice in a packed Berlin underground train! The picture fits stereotype groupings of "uncultured and primitive" immigrants. This misunderstanding is further enhanced by the usage of generalised terminologies of African dances, African food... Many times I have asked myself why one cannot categorically say "we are inviting you to eat Senegalese food". Each country in Africa is unique and rich in culture and we should be proud to exhibit such a rich and diverse heritage. Such terminologies only enhance the magnitude of ignorance about our continent, or how do you otherwise define a recent situation in Berlin that was reported in a local newspaper, that donors met and donated two hundred Euros to assist educational projects in Africa? In Africa, a continent of 53 nations and massive countries, remember a country like Sudan is as big as western Europe and a game park in Kenya, Tsavo by name, is as big as Belgium. So why not mention the country you are assisting, it makes the whole situation unfathomable for informed thinking minds! To ordinary Germans, Africa is one country at war, and ravaged by starvation. Interesting to note too is that when development agencies are soliciting for aid, they have pictures of some of the ugliest Africans I have ever seen! One is left wondering whether this is a silent Western policy of stigmatizing the continent. Any society has beautiful and ugly people, that's why the words exist. How come the west choose beautiful models in their advertisements, yet they pick the ugliest when they need an African picture! Please tell me am wrong or is it this monkey- looking image that fits the stereotype? Please don't misunderstand me! I am not biased about my people, but the truth must be told simple and clear. Some of my words might seem to be painful. I am not ethnocentric, I respect cultures but I don't respect cultures which marginalise groups.

Back to my African warriors! These men come from cultures which see the woman as inferior and they are the bosses. Right or wrong, their opinion is always right because of the simple fact that they are men! It amuses me to see them pushing baby prams or children's wagons, sharing domestic work, since they want to live in Europe, that is the price they have to pay. A Kiswahili saying goes "Mtaka cha mvunguni sharti einame" - He who needs something on the floor must bend", and they surely do! A German woman cannot understand why her jobless husband, who spend the whole day watching television while she was at work, cannot help her with domestic chores. The African man too is unable to understand what the German woman is complaining about, since half of his lifetime he lived in rural Kenya where the men idle in the local market and the women do all the domestic and farm work. Yet his father, at the end of the coffee harvest and delivery to the mills, goes to collect the coffee check and the wife has no right to ask how the money is spend even if she worked on "his farm". Mind you, statistics show that women in Africa own less than one percent of the land, but produce 80 percent of the food. For this ordinary Safari Partner the German woman is only petty and spoiled! In fact she is denying him what is naturally right, his position in society as a man. And believe me, for their ego it is painful. After attaining German papers, such men "abandon the yoke of slavery", go back to their villages and marry women of their cadre who need no education to know their rightful place, the kitchen! Back home they play the role of a successful African man abroad! They make sure they come home with an imported car and decorate themselves with gold chains to display their "success" in Europe. It is a false picture, but a sure ticket of getting a beautiful bride to "the land of plenty!" Victims of such unions fall into what I would term as "a trap of immigration illusions and conmen". It is a commonly told story in Nigeria and Ghana. When such women come to Europe, they rarely integrate into the German society, their husbands, who also don't speak good German, intentionally do not make an effort to make them learn the language. These African warriors make sure that heir wives remain in African social groups to avoid them being "polluted" by western cultures. The husbands only show such women what is relevant to their role as African wives and mothers, namely African shops and African churches. Personally I would call such places not a continental meeting point, but a Ghanaian or a Nigerian shop, for our food cuisines in Africa differ just like the way Italian dishes differ from the Russian ones! Some of these girls stay with their African warriors, but others are known to run away after "opening" their eyes!

On the other hand, Kenyans stick to or change their Mzungu partners. Unlike in the West African community, it is almost unheard of to see a Kenyan woman married to a Kenyan man in Germany. This too has its cultural and historical reasons. Due to strong western influence and especially tourism, Kenyans living in Germany meet their partners in the tourism industry. At home it is generally accepted that marrying a white man is a step to financial success. The majority of Kenyans who marry German tourists come from social disadvantaged classes, thus minimising the chances of marrying their own who in most cases cannot offer them the lifestyle they desire. Don't be surprised if you hear Kenyans laughing at their own for having come to Europe and marrying a black man, for a Nigerian hard to understand, but in Kenya a norm. Black and black relationships between Kenyans are commonly found among the student community in America and Britain, but sorry, not in Germany.

For ten years I have lived here and I only know one case in Frankfurt. This "unique Kenyan couple" also comes from an affluent family. In fact, here it is easy to know where an African mother pushing a baby pram comes from, by only taking a glance at the colour of her child!That is if you are not colour blind like the recent reports by some German journalists who keep on referring to Obama, a child born of black and white parents as black yet he is coloured! Coloured children with black mothers are mainly from Kenyan, Ugandan and Tanzanian, whereas black children are born of West African parents, mainly Nigeria and Ghana. Most Kenyan girls have a first black child too, born in Kenya, and a coloured child from their "safari partner".

Back to my Kofi. Judging from the above background, I was only another Kenyan girl to him, eager to land in the hands of a white man. Kofi never chewed his words on Kenyan women. He told me his counterparts from West Africa were always surprised that women from East Africa always wanted to marry white men, I quote: "Kenya girl like to marry this your Mzungu oh" He asked me bitterly what Kenyan women saw in white men. He said, no West African woman would want to live like Kenyans. "You know, my sister, if you really know what brought you to Europe you'll never marry a white man. These white people want to be with you all the time, when will you ever earn money and send to your relatives back home?" Kofi asked.

I understand Kofi and his mentality, but what I fail to understand is his failure to ask me what I was doing in Germany. He only assumed that I had come to Germany through a German tourist, like the majority of Kenyans in Germany, Kenya being a tourists' country. I also don't blame Kofi and people who think like him. But what Kofi failed to know then is that I come from a country which has both, economic and political stability. Kenyans only go to foreign countries for educational purposes and it is a national pride to come back after the completion of their studies. So you can imagine the shock I got when I saw a fellow African, proud and excited about owning a foreign citizenship. It was a pity that we were talking on different wavelengths, as we say in journalism.

All this time while we were talking on the balcony, “the brothers and sisters” were partying, everybody was in high spirits. The high sound of music played in this room reminded me of my student days at the University of Nairobi. Little did I know that this was a common habit of Africans living here, why, I don’t know, but I guess a lot of it has to do with owning stereo players for the first time in their lives. The sad thing is that some Germans who have never travelled to Africa think that is how Africans behave in their countries, what a pity! And what a distortion of a continent’s image. I think Germany’s integration problems are dominated by misinformation and stereotypes. I also noticed that Kofi’s neighbour, a German, was staring at us from an adjacent balcony. When Kofi realised that I was not interested in his generous offer, he saluted his neighbour whom he referred to as “Kalle”. The rest of the conversation was in German, but I later came to learn that he welcomed him to join the party.

It was this neighbour who would later turn out to be the father of my son.

From the kind of background I have described, one can excuse Kofi’s offer as generous. To him I did not have to be a sexual doll or a cleaning woman, he was only offering me “a future in the promised land on a silver plate”. To him and his gang this was a golden opportunity and only a stupid Kenyan would turn down such a chance in exchange of a Mzungu (white man). I don’t blame Kofi, come to think of it! When I look at the call-girls and Beach boys in the Kenyan coastal towns of Malindi and Mombasa, the way they toil to catch a mzungu or a rich German, or are not all Germans rich? The slums they live in, compare them to the “lucky” ones who have caught a German, their lives are different. Here they can live in a clean apartment and even if the man is not working they can still afford to eat.

So is that not paradise? I understand Kofi, but I am afraid he might not understand me.

KALLE

Kalle joined the African party as invited by Kofi. He was in his mid-thirties, black hair and had what Germans refer to as a "Bierbauch", a "beer stomach". As time went by, Kalle requested Kofi to talk to me.

Our conversation was not easy, for he could not speak English, but I later came to know from one of the translators that he was a mechanical engineer. I don't know whether it was lack of proper English, but years later I came to know what my "Ghanaian brother" referred to as engineer was a mechanic!

Kalle was very excited to meet me, for he claimed Kenya was his dream. According to him, he had for years dreamed of visiting Kenya and meeting a live Kenyan was partly his dream come true. He later warned me not to spend a night at Kofi's flat if I was not his girlfriend. Though I found this strange, I did not ask him why. I only told him that I had no intentions of sleeping there. I later came to learn from him that Kofi was an African Casanova who never wasted an opportunity to lay naive and desperate African women immigrants in Germany.

According to Kalle, if an African girl overstayed in Kofi's flat without his interests, he threw her out and it was not a rare occurrence to see the unwelcome girls' clothes being thrown down from Kofi's balcony. Whether this narration was true or meant to scare me away from Kofi, I will never know.

What I know is that after this meeting with Kalle I never saw Kofi again, but I kept meeting Kalle. Call it a relationship, but we sort of developed in interest on each other. Come August and I had to leave for Kenya.

For Kalle I was now his girlfriend, but for me, I was only having fun and trying to forget my troubled relationship in Kenya.

Back home I was in a relationship with a businessman and politician who kept me on my toes emotionally. Though rich, the man was not educated and he never wasted time to remind me of this gap between us. It was a burden for our relationship, more so because I was known in many of his circles due to my work. It shook the core of his African manhood. I will never forget one evening when we went for dinner at the Intercontinental Hotel in Nairobi. In the Hotel lobby we met some his political colleagues who were so full of praise for me for war reports I had made in Ruanda during the genocide. He later ruined the whole evening and sulked, "where will I ever take you where you are not known". I knew that the only alternative to continue this relationship would have been to quit my job, and you can be sure that's why I opted to flirt with Kalle.
Kalle and I visited each other often. I knew very little about this man, except that he had lived in Berlin for ten years, came from Saarbrücken and loved big motorbikes. He also told me that he had a son with an alcoholic woman. He never told me, though, whether when he met the woman she was an alcoholic or if he turned her into one. He only said that the situation was so bad that his son had to be taken care of by the woman's cousin.
Anyway, his life never interested me for as far as I knew this man was not my type. From the short time I had known Kalle, I realised that we had nothing in common. His lifestyle, clothing, interests and so on were not my thing. I love older men with affluent lives and more importantly, men with intellectual capabilities and Kalle was none of these.
A week before I left Germany, I realised that like any other African returning home, I had excess luggage. The shopping had consumed all the money I had and since I had Kalle as a friend, I asked for his financial help. To my surprise Kalle told me that he had no money, not that I needed much, but the tone in which he answered me back was unfriendly. I was really shocked and this he saw from my expression. When I look back I can now accept that this was my first "Safari Partner cultural shock". Anyway, he said he could only afford to give me fifty

Deutsch Marks, but he insisted that I should refund him when he came to Kenya. For sure, I should have told him to go to hell. After all, don't men in Kenya take pride in helping their women? Surely, this was a cultural shock for me. Our cultures put women in both privileged and exploitable situations. Although women have attained some degree of emancipation in Kenya, it is not a surprise to find a man paying all the bills even if his woman is earning more, it is seen as normal, and in some parts a man whose bills are put up by his woman is seen as a lesser man! So don't be surprised if you marry a white man and he insists that you share the house bills! All my life I had met men who took pride in spending money on women and here was a man, a mzungu, as we call them in Kenya, a white man, telling me to refund him fifty marks! What the devil had I met? In Kenya there were those prostitutes living in big villas and driving big cars, bought by their German boyfriends and here was one telling me to refund him fifty Marks. The mentality in my country is that if you have a mzungu, you are a rich woman. As if that was not enough, Kalle seemed withdrawn and later that afternoon I heard him murmur to himself: "If the plane crashes when I am coming to Kenya then my fifty Marks will be lost forever."

I swear to God, I am not exaggerating, but this is a mzungu I met. Mwikali, a long-term girlfriend of mine, warned me never to ignore small problems at the beginning of a relationship in the hope that they will vanish. Most people do and I tell you from experience, those are wishful thoughts. I think if we don't ignore such small problems we can save ourselves a lot of pain and tears in the future, but you know, most of us never learn.
From this kind of behaviour I would have fast learned and saved myself from a lot of pain. It was the stuff dreams were made of, and not easily won. Kalle's silent murmur shocked me but I ignored it. My present priority was to pay for my luggage and get on with my life. Reality was for tomorrow!

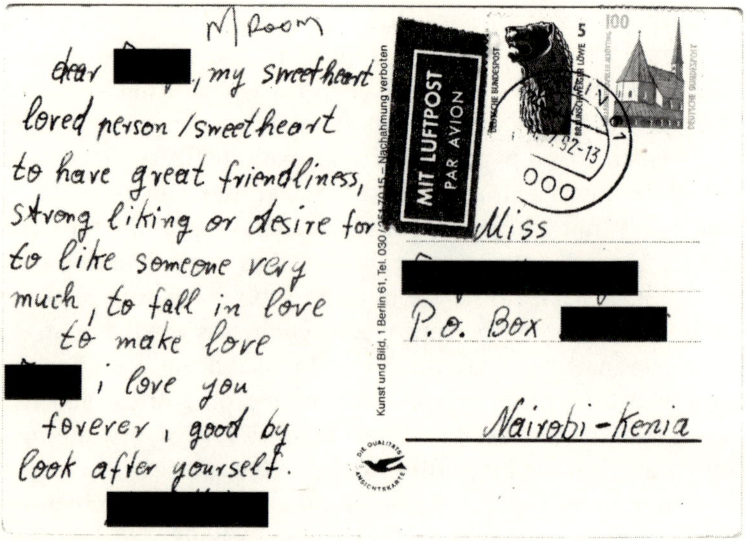
M Room
dear [redacted], my sweetheart
loved person / sweetheart
to have great friendliness,
strong liking or desire for
to like someone very
much, to fall in love
to make love
[redacted] i love you
forever, good by
look after yourself.
[redacted]

MIT LUFTPOST
PAR AVION

Miss
[redacted]
P.O. Box [redacted]
Nairobi-Kenia

Some of the unsealed vulgar written cards
Kalle send to me in my place of work!

On my arrival in Kenya, he kept on sending me postcards written in German and broken English, but what caught my attention with these cards was not the quantity, for I could receive ten cards a week, but the contents. Some of the cards had such vulgar language and mind you, they were not sealed in an envelope and they were sent to my working place where I was a senior editor! You should have seen the look on the messenger's face when he brought them to my desk! Even a school-going pupil knows some things need privacy! What the hell had I gotten myself into?

December 1992 one evening Kalle landed at the Jomo Kenyatta Airport, Nairobi.

For Kalle this was his dream, he was in Kenya for the first time, the land of his dreams, Kenya, where giraffes and elephants mingled with humans in the streets or did the television in Germany lie? He was already too excited and eager to see

live migrations of animals from the famous Serengeti National Park to the Massai Mara game reserve, and even so he was going to see a life Massai warrior! Call it a dream come true.
Though not allowed, I went with my official car to pick up my mzungu with the support of our TV-news crew driver Murigi, who was as excited as Kalle. After all his colleague had travelled to Germany and met a mzungu who was now coming to visit her. Wasn't that a dream for many? Having a mzungu to many Kenyans means wealth and happiness, more so a German, or weren't all Germans rich? The colonialists had left this myth, the German tourists enforced it, the scores of diplomats in Nairobi and the Kenyans married to mzungus have maintained it. What these Kenyans never tell is that mzungus too have their shortfalls. Like any other human being, not every mzungu is romantic and rich. It is true that the mzungus, unlike many Africans, rarely beat their wives and those who do go to prison. What some of our people don't know is that this harmony has been created by both, men and women, legal institutions and governments and above all the realisation that all men, women included, are equal before the law.
Equal education for all creates this awareness, it is not the color that transforms a human being to a gentleman. I feel it is important to treat all children as equal, give them equal opportunities and eradicate the myth of the superior white civilisation.
If the Africans don't educate their daughters, then the African man will always feel superior, for he has the education, hence the financial power, he will beat his illiterate wife who has neither money nor the information to take him to court, thus creating this bad picture of an African man who is a woman's survival kit and a tyrant. Men of all colors can be romantic and gentle if they are dealing with equal partners of the same wealth, education and so forth. Sorry, my gender crusade sometimes takes control of me! Where was I before I started my equality crusade. Yeah, I wanted to say that Kalle arrived in Kenya.

I took him to the 680 Hotel where we stayed for a week before we proceeded to the coastal town of Mombasa. In this one week I had already noticed a character trait in Kalle that I had never seen before. This was because I was spending day and night with him.

I noticed that he lost his temper on very minor things. At one time he shouted at me at the top of his voice because I had, according to him, "forced" him to wear a shirt which was too warm. Honestly, I only gave him a suggestion, for being a TV-personality, I cared what he wore. I did not want to walk in the streets of Nairobi with a mzungu dressed like a hitch-hiking student on a holiday! You should have seen him yelling at me at the hotel's dining room. It was really embarrassing for me. To my disgust the waiter ran to us, thinking that he had brought the wrong food. As usual with Kenyan waiters, he was extremely concerned about offending a mzungu, something which irritates me. I should state here that it is a common practice in Kenya to see waiters giving more attention to white tourists and snubbing their African customers. It is also known occurrence to see Kenyan waiters in big hotels ignoring African customers and more so women. Though this might sound absurd, it is a common occurrence with a historical, colonial and chauvinistic background. To make matters worse, women are known to be sent out of Kenyan hotels if they are not accompanied by men. The mentality being that unaccompanied women are prostitutes and a nuisance for male tourists. I must mention here that prostitution is illegal in Kenya, though practised. It is one of those "evils" like abortion, homosexuality and paedophilia which the government wishes away, ever heard of the ostrich burying its head in the sand? What some of these waiters forget is that Kenyan women work and have a right to enjoy their money. I am not saying it is a daily discrimination occurrence but it happens in some hotels. What is interesting to note is that these waiters don't discriminate white female clients, after all the mentality being that white people are rich.

The current U:S:A president elect Barrack Obama while visiting his relatives in Kenya was too a victim of this attitude. In one of Nairobi noble Restaurant he and his sister Dr. Auma ombama were unnecessarily kept waiting for 30 minutes ye a white American couple who arrived after them was swiftly served!

The shirt saga was not the end of the story. Like any good Kenyan I invited one of my editors, a Mr. Kamutu, for an evening meal. We ordered a Kenyan meal composed of spiced brown rice (Pilau), special hot vegetables called kachubari, composed of tomatoes, coriander, lemon and onions, and roast beef popularly known as “nyama choma”. All went well until my colleague went to the toilet. Kalle looked at me like a lion and roared. He complained about my colleague eating too many vegetables, leaving not enough for him! My God, in a normal situation I would only have laughed, but it was already getting too much for me. We were in a hotel where we could order more food and those of you who know Kenyan culture and generosity would be shocked by such levels of greediness. I had no words for this man and his class. I tried to cool Kalle down for I did not want embarrassment for the second time in a day, worse still in front of my boss. What kind of man had I gotten myself into?. Only then I realised that I was dealing with one of the complicated and primitive mzungus on earth, and the sooner he went back to Germany, the better for me.

I had taken three weeks leave to show Kalle around and I had promised myself to do it, however hard it was getting. After the vegetable and shirt saga we proceeded to the Ocean View Beach Hotel in Mombasa. We boarded the antique Safari steam train in Nairobi. The arrangement fitted Kalle’s African fantasies, the well-kept beds in the first class wagon, the friendly waiters and the board restaurant with its exotic cuisines. The sprouting Kaviti plains, Savannah grassland decorated by nature with a variety of gazelles, giraffes, zebras, and buffaloes, really the rich unique Kenyan wildlife. Acacia trees, looking like nature umbrellas, the Mighty and Holy Baobab (miamba) along Masimba and Mtitu, all mesmerised him and the view of the snow-capped Kilimanjaro Mountain from Voi was indescribable! Scores of Monkeys near Voi! Then we neared the coastal region of Kenya at Mazeiras, the beauty of the coconut trees was breathtaking. Kalle fell in love with the white sandy beaches and the tons of food cooked at the hotel. He could not believe the beauty of the clear blue waters of the Indian Ocean when we strolled on Diani Beach. The whispering-like coconuts trees, the nature wonder of Diani Reef, even the German television documentaries could not match what he was witnessing in Kenya! For him a holiday of a lifetime, but for me a nightmare. On the 4th of January 1993 we went for an early morning swim, our spirits were high and when we came back to the hotel, Kalle made love to me, for the first time in our relationship without a condom. Call it the genies of Mombasa, to this date I have never understood why I did what I did. I knew very well that this Mzungu was an adventure, but I somehow did not think I could get pregnant! Crazy, is it not? Don't worry, I have paid a big price for that minute of carelessness!

None of us thought of the consequences at that time, but this was the procreation of my beloved son Matata.

On January 15th of the same year, Kalle went back to Berlin. For me the departure was the end of the chapter of our relationship. I had realised that I had met the wrong mzungu, I had no time for a man who was always nervous and shouting, but above all we had no common interests.

On going back to Germany Kalle was in love. He kept on sending me postcards which I never replied to, but he never gave up. For me this was history, but for him his life had just begun. He wrote letters telling me to resign my job and come to live with him in Germany. I declined the offer.

My monthly periods are very irregular. Since Kalle had left Kenya, I had not received my periods but to me this was not a surprise. I can stay for three to four months without getting my periods. Surprisingly I never thought myself pregnant, sounds naive but that's me.

Two months after Kalle had returned to Germany, I fainted in the middle of a press conference in Treasury Building. Later in the day, Mwikali, my school time girlfriend, suggested that I see a gynaecologist. At first I asked her why the gyno? But she said, "Tara, you could be pregnant". True to her suspicion, the gyno found that I was two months pregnant. Talking of shock! Since my highschool days I told my mother that I would never get married, never have babies, but that I would devote my life to my career. Ten years later I was still of the same opinion.

In fact the gyno realised that I was not excited about his announcement. To his surprise I answered: "I have never wanted a baby in my lifetime." He only said that I was a unique patient, for all his time in practice he had never met an African woman who never wanted to have a child in her lifetime. All the same he encouraged me to accept the baby, something I only did then because I was scared of performing an abortion.

THE BIRTH OF MATATA

After being pronounced pregnant, my maternal instincts encouraged me to maintain the relationship with the mzungu. Not because of the relationship, but because of now the presence of a child. I came from a broken family and I wanted to offer my child a better background, call it wishful thinking! To this date I have always felt guilty of "choosing" the wrong father for my son. However much I try to reason, it is an injustice I did to my son, my naivety and wild attributes went too far!

In May 1993 I travelled to Berlin for the second time, this time to get to know the father of my child. Kalle tried to show his best but his weird character traits would emerge from time to time. I came back after a month's holiday, feeling sad and guilty, guilty that I had made a baby with the wrong man and more so feeling that I had chosen the wrong person to be the father of

my child. All the same I decided to put more energy on taking care of my pregnancy.
On October 10th, 1993, usually a public holiday in Kenya, Matata was born in Mater Hospital. It was a smooth labour, despite the fears I had had on the process. Part of the reason of my early life why I never wanted to have a child was fear of the labour pains. Other women who had talked about this process scared the wit out of me, with the stories of unbearable pain. To be honest, what I felt during child's birth was bearable, not to mention that I could afford to read in the intervals, to the amazement of the nurses, Muthoni Likimani's novel "What does a man want?".
I must mention here Kalle's reaction to my pregnancy. He informed me that he was happy about it. Whether he said this to please me, I'll never know. My employer's insurance policy never covered pregnancy costs, so I had to take care of my bills at the hospital. To my surprise Kalle never helped me with the same. To add injury to insult, he never telephoned to congratulate me. Not that it surprised me from his past behaviours, but it only hurt me more. Years later, when I castigated him on the same he said he hadn't been able to afford to call me, for it was expensive to call from Germany. Today when I stupidly incur high telephone bills, calling my relatives in Kenya, I wonder why a man cannot pick up the telephone and incur a five Euro bill to congratulate a woman who has born him a child. Yet he spends two times that amount daily on cigarettes. It is really a puzzling world!
Where mzungus not caring? How come I had one who could not help me? Weren't there mzungus supporting Kenyan women with children who they had never fathered? As time went by, I became bitter and bitterer and hundreds of questions haunted me.
The same year Kalle came to Kenya, many of my friends had thought that the mzungu had come to see his newborn son, but deep in my own mind I knew very well that Kalle was coming for a holiday.

To add injury to insult, when he arrived he was only carrying his holiday bag, not a single present for his newborn baby! In his pocket he was carrying a thousand Deutsch Mark, which he made no mistake by "declaring" on arrival that it was enough for his coffee outings at the coffee shop in Mama Ngina Street. He also chewed no words by telling me that if any money remained, he would take it back to Berlin, for he did not want to starve on arrival! I swear I am not exaggerating, what a man!! What sin did I commit to warrant such a treatment and relationship. Here was a man who took what many yearn for granted. He comes to Kenya with only a thousand marks in his pocket, has free residence, a free cook in my house, free meals, a free car and driver and on top of all a baby who he does not care a bit to know what it eats, about its clothes or its medical care. Many a times I asked myself what fate had in store for me. Did I really deserve this? How could this man be so unfair, was he naive or just mean-sick?

After my son was born I took care of all expenses and the father did nothing. It was only the grandmother of my son in Germany who used to send clothes for her grandson once in a while, it used to touch and really pain me.

Again and again I asked myself, of all people, how I could land into such trouble, not that I was special but I had all the chances of meeting at least decent and responsible people, black or white.

Through my job as a television reporter, I had met people from all walks of life, street peddlers to senior politicians and academics, mention all, yet the only person who fathered my son was a dubious, nervous wreck. Talk of life's mystery or is it just destiny?

After one month Kalle went back to Germany. This time my mind was made up and I decided to do the best to bring up my son as a single parent. I also resumed work and made all efforts to forget the shadow of the father of my son.

One year after I decided to try a new relationship with a Cameroonian diplomat whom I had met in the course of my job. The relationship went on for years and I owe him a reat deal in helping me mentally and financially in bringing up my son, up to this day we are still in constant touch.

In April 1997 I talked intensely to my Cameroonian friend about the future of my son. Much as we liked each other, we never saw a future together. His past life was more complicated than mine, though that is relative. He was a single parent with five children from three different women and I never wasted time in telling him that he had already too much on his hands. Moreover, I told him that I could not see a promising future for him to bring up my child in case I died. Though this sounds unfair, it has some social background. I am not saying that my friend was irresponsible, but I was only looking at the situation on the basis of probability.

Supposing I married my friend and later migrated to Cameroon, then I died, what would happen to my son? A colored child with two black parents! If you don't know the African mentality, you might not understand this. I don't want to use strong words, but in Africa besides tribal prejudice we also have racial biases, call it African style racism.

The belief is that a decent African woman does not have sexual relationships with white men. It is believed that – and believe me, in a great deal – that colored children are born of prostitute mothers. Such children are discriminated against and they bear their bulk of abuses in school. Worse, if you are poor and take the child to a normal school. Most people in Nairobi take their colored children to international schools where there is a mixture of children from affluent backgrounds. Woe unto you if you cannot afford it, for your child will be scolded "how come your mother slept with a white man?" or "son of Malaya" (prostitute). It is even worse to see a colored child riding on public transport. Though not loudly vindicated, you notice the look on people's faces like "how come this one got a child with a mzungu who cannot buy a car?". Worse still if you live in cheap estates, people would be wondering why you don't live in rich residential areas, the likes of Dahlem in Berlin. Believe me, if you live in the poor districts of Nairobi, chances are that you would be attacked by thieves often, for they think a mother of colored child has money from the mzungu father! The situation in Nairobi is worsened because of a big diplomatic community, international investors and remember, the United Nations headquarters on environment, UNEP, is based in Nairobi. Most of our neighbours are at war and all peacekeepers, development agencies and the international press reside in Nairobi. Such foreigners lead exorbitant lifestyles due to the strength of their foreign currency, giving the impression that white people are rich. It is a myth that is hard to erase!

Take for example a girl I met here in Berlin, she toiled for eight good years making beds in hotels to meet these standards and at least afford her a holiday for herself, her daughter and her jobless husband. Instead of saving the money she earned from her back-breaking manual hotel job, she had to go to her home village once a year to show off how she had married a rich white man. At one time she even hosted and financed a traditional wedding ceremony, giving the impression that "the rich husband had come to pay dowry". This gesture is in African tradition unheard of, a woman paying her dowry and the jobless German must have later laughed himself silly at this pretentious show of wealth. If only the poor villagers had known the money they were feasting on was hard-earned and that the allegedly rich son-in-law was jobless and penniless! These are just but some of the expectations of having sired a child with a white man. To date many Africans still believe that all white people are rich. What a misconception! When I walk through the Zoologischer Garten area in Berlin and see all those homeless and hungry people, I only wonder how impossible that picture is to contemplate in my motherland! I have always wondered when I see what the reality is in Europe, that here people have to toil to earn a living, in contrast to the belief of many in Africa. The

reality here is, nobody collects money from the German streets and people have to work hard to survive.
Woe onto you if you live in Europe and you are not rich! The "lucky" Africans who manoeuvred their way to Europe are also affected by the same mentality predicament. Back home, the expectations are as high as Mount Kilimanjaro! And woe onto you if you come here and don't keep your dozen or so relatives back home comfortable, woe onto you if you don't import a Mercedes for your relatives in Africa, don't build a house or bring your relatives to Europe for a holiday, then you are a failure! The above are the "laid" standards to measure a successful African abroad! Whoever laid down these standards should have come here first and you know such standards have driven many of us to ruin. Taking into consideration that most foreigners from tourist destinations like Kenya and Thailand who come to Germany are a result of sex tourism, people with little or no education, in order to meet the above standards they either have to turn to crime like drug selling or the sexual trade. And you know, the victims are even too happy to meet these expectations at whatever cost, life is a mystery!
Whenever I narrate my suffering to my people while on holiday most of them are astounded. Some even think I am creating the story in order not to share with them my "massive" wealth made in Germany! One of them, a natural comedian, Kingangi nicknamed "Cha Waters alias Crocodile", once asked: "Hey, come on Tara, tell us the truth, which Germany did you go to? All the people who live in Germany are rich, yet you come here with stories of suffering, you must have gone to the wrong country."
Some years ago, a leading Kenyan television team, visiting the famous tourist fair ITB in Berlin, did a documentary on me where I discussed some of these issues. They too filmed on my daily undertakings in a programme known as "my day with you..." Interesting is that the same year I went home and a clerk at the Bank, while serving me, noticed who I was and exclaimed "if people who suffer in Germany look the way you do,

then I don't mind coming there!" The myth of rich Europe has its background. When the colonialists came to Africa, they built massive Victorian villas and lived wealthily. In Kenya, for example, a story is told of a rich farmer, Lord Delamere, of how he in the early 1960s used to boast that he could line up money coins from Mombasa to Nairobi, a distance of about 500 kilometres. After colonialism and rich land settlers came the diplomats and businessmen, who lived exorbitantly, too. Some of them married Africans and their lifestyle was a dream to many, new four wheel cars, houses with swimming pools etc. Then came the tourist boom in Kenya. British and German tourists dominate the scene to this day. They too enhanced the myth of the rich west, lived in expensive hotels, a lifestyle middle level Kenyans could only dream of, and to crown it all, some of these tourists, as old as 70 years, married 19- year-old Kenyans, bought them flashy cars, built expensive houses for the in-laws and... While educated Kenyans women and men were busy working in offices, the poor Kenyan women and men without education were on the beaches, busy looking for tourists for survival. Through these contacts emerged the first group of colored children born of prostitutes. With this kind of background, the seeds of western wealth myth and colored children born of prostitutes were sown, and the roots are deep and it is hard to tell ordinary third world citizens that you are poor in Europe, or that you married a white out of love and not for money! It is trying to erase the impossible!
Anyway, to cut a long story short, I decided to leave my job voluntarily and migrated to Germany. The main reason being my son's future. Then there was no media freedom in Kenya. We were demotivated, censured and underpaid. Professional journalism in my station was a dream then, the then government of president Moi controlled information with an iron fist. Our news slot was fifteen minutes. You could toil the whole day gathering reports and shortly before you went on air, the then presidential press unit could come with a presidential story long enough to cover the 15 minutes newstime. They had their own

newscaster too, and he had to be a man. According to the Moi government, a man's voice was more respected by the patriarchal masses, more so when it centred on propaganda or so they believed! One of my colleagues, who later migrated to Canada, revealed to me that she was the only lady newscaster allowed to read the presidential bulletin. The reason being that her father intervened, for he came from the same tribe as the president and worked in State house as a driver! African governments! It was a nightmare for many of us. No wonder when the next government licensed new media houses, almost all my former workmates left our employer. It was like an exodus. Unfortunately for me, I had already left to the land of Mercedes! It hurts me to know that a selfish opposition politician used my departure to castigate his rival, who was the information minister I had been working for, in parliament. He claimed that I left due to job mobbing, namely sexual harassment, by the information minister. It was not true, my leaving voluntarily.

LIFE IN BERLIN – 1997

The time my son was three years old, he was a handsome happy boy despite the uncertainty of his life. He had a loving mother and that mattered. What he did not know was that he had a father who in my opinion was weird. Up to now Kalle had made several holidays to Kenya, repeating the same behaviours. At the age of 3, Matata had not received a bar of chocolate or a present from his father.

All this time Kalle was begging me to join him in Germany. When I made up my mind to leave, I received a letter from him assuring me that he would send us a ticket to Berlin. Come the day and there was no ticket! Honestly this did not surprise me. I believe that everybody has their small secrets, except for my closest girlfriend Mwikali, nobody else knew about the woes affecting my relationship with the mzungu. The only thing I received from Kalle was a letter apologising for not having sent a ticket on the ground of poverty. Mind you, by this time I had sold all my household goods, ready to leave for Germany, think of the inconveniences! He claimed that he had lost his job with VARTA and had no hope of getting money. As if to slap me in the face, he said that he had only money for his food and that life in Germany was very expensive, "Essen und Trinken ist teuer in Deutschland", as if in Nairobi we collect food from the streets or manna from heaven!

And if that was not enough, he asked me if I had money to spare to buy the ticket. Sure, I was a working class and independent modern African woman and I would even have bought a ticket were it not his idea to buy one, so I bought a ticket! Honestly I did not seem to have a lot of choices, I had left my job, and my pride would not allow me to keep on, being fed by my friend. At least if I left for Germany, I would not have to worry about rent, quality school for my son and so on. At least in Germany, or so I believed, I would not have nosy neighbours by the virtue of having a mzungu child. The other alternative was to look for a job. Unfortunately then, unlike today, there was only one broadcasting station in Kenya and the government had the monopoly of the electronic media. So I opted to leave.

April 1997 my son and I arrived at Berlin Tegel Airport. Because of Kalle not sending me the ticket, I decided not to tell him of my arrival. I called him on arrival, but he was not at home. To make matters worse, he had no answering machine. From 10 o'clock in the morning, we finally managed to get Kalle at 6 in the evening. My son was already too tired, not to mention the boredom of staying that long at the airport.

When Kalle arrived, the only thing I remember him saying was that he had to board a bus to Neukölln for he had no money for taxi. It took us several hours to get there, for Kalle had to keep changing buses and asking passengers which bus went to Neukölln from Tegel. To me this was funny, for I assumed there must be a map to direct passengers to their destinations in such a city.

Berlin 1997, Matata taking a nap in his corner in Kalles one room flat.

Today I know the efficient Berlin transport network, and to imagine a man who lives in this city and does not know that there is a direct train not far from the Airport to where he lived, says more than words of his calibre! 8 hours waiting at the Airport, loss of direction, changing buses more than 5 times, boxes in hand, tired... that is how I started my life in Berlin.
We arrived in Kalle's new residence in Rudow in the district of Neukölln. We were tired and it was a relief to have somewhere to lie down after the long trip and wait at the airport.
However, on arrival I was shocked to notice that my friend was living in a single room, 40 sqm, to be precise. Not that I expected a villa, but in the letters he had sent me to Kenya he had glorified his new apartment. Here we were at last, having left a five-bedroom house in the Lavington district of Nairobi (those of you who don't know Nairobi: Lavington is a noble district in Nairobi). So that was it. I later came to learn that the district we were living was like the "Ghetto" of Berlin and in Europe one notices such areas because of the high storey buildings. Neu-

kölln has the highest percentage of unemployment in Berlin and the highest amount of anti-social behaviours that accompany poor urban dwellers. The district has a high immigrant population, too, so there I was, Tara the ambitious village girl that turned society girl in Nairobi, now falling down to the lowest social cadre! So you can imagine the shock I got when I realised that we had come to live in Europe in a place where we had no bedroom, let alone a bed.

All the same I explained to my son that it was normal for the father to live in such a place, for he was alone and in due time we would get a bigger place. Kalle himself was excited, lost for words for seeing us, and despite what I have always referred to as his weird character, he was in his best moods.

Shortly he suggested that he had a mattress in the cellar which Matata could use in the meantime, a suggestion I found o.k..

Two days in Berlin and my friend could not hide his real behaviour for long. He started getting jittery, shouting and at times screaming to the detriment of his neighbours, if not us. He wasted no time in writing his house code of ethics and pinning them in the kitchen. Everywhere there were pieces of paper full of his house code of ethics!

He minced no words in telling me to educate my son not to go and disturb him while he was eating. He also told me that "my son" had no business blocking his pathway to the kitchen with his toys. He screamed loud if his feet came across a toy. His behaviour was like a sharp knife in my heart.

With time the situation went from bad to worse, and I started to look forward to the time he left the house for school. I must mention here that Kalle had stopped work and in order to get the government allowance for being jobless, he had to register with a labour college for some training in sanitation. So he used to leave the house at five in the morning until four in the evening, a time I looked forward to, for I did not know anybody else in Berlin who I could go to. Hard to believe, but coming from top society and British Kenya, I found myself crying one morning after Kalle had left for his training and all this drama because of a dress code!. I was ready to accept Kalles social cadre, but I had not realised fully what it entailed. On this particular day I observed my "future husband" leave the house in a workman's blue overall and bread with salami packed in a lunchbox. The reality hit home. Never before had I known anybody in my closer circle who did not go to work in tailor- made suits and briefcase. The people I knew back home met in flashy restaurants with buffets for lunch, but did not carry lunch in a bag! We have a Kiswahili saying which goes "Mpanda Ngazi hushuka", meaning he who climbs a ladder comes down. All meant to prepare you for changes in life, but it seemed I was not yet there. Believe me, I wept bitterly and little did I know that the worst was yet to come. To me this was the end of the world, the reality hit home and believe me, it signalled the end of my familiar lifestyle and dreams. For an ordinary German hard to understand, but for me an extreme change!

With time I met some Africans who showed me a park where I began spending the days with my son. Though I thought this would break the stress at "home", Kalle wasted no time in telling me that I had to come home before six and even added, "My mother is shocked that instead of spending time with me you are always out". Unfortunately at this time the mother never knew the reason for not being at home. However, I wasted no time in telling him that I never knew his mother and in any case what she thought of me was irrelevant. One summer afternoon he sarcastically suggested that since I was always in Hasenheide Park and using the train, I could use his monthly ticket when he came home instead of buying one and wasting money. I found it a welcome idea which I was later to badly regret.

A week went by using his ticket and as bad luck would have it, I misplaced what I would now prefer to call "Kalle's precious ticket". The ticket was misplaced in one of the small pockets in my Versace handbag and when I could not produce it on time, Kalle's temper went out of control. He screamed at the top of his voice, kicked anything that he could find on his way, banged his television with the fists and used his favourite word

"I am not a millionaire, I cannot afford to buy two tickets in a month and if you don't find my ticket I am going to kill you tonight". Though my son could not understand what his father was saying, he naturally sensed that something was very wrong. Within all the chaos my son started crying at the top of his voice and telling the father to stop beating the mother. This was after the father threw his house shoes in my face. Up to this day I have never seen my son so sad, and for the first time since his birth Matata could not sleep up to midnight. He kept on crying in spells while lying on his mattress and pointing at his father. This picture and the red and white pullover my son wore on that day still remain fresh in my mind.

In less than an hour I had found the misplaced ticket and quietly handed it over to the owner. The submissive manner in which I handed it over reminded me of the many women undergoing domestic violence in Kenya. The once bold Tara, champion of women rights, an aspiring politician in the Nairobi Westlands before the departure to Germany and a holder of a certificate of participation from the women's conference in Beijing, China, was now a victim of domestic violence! And not even in Africa, but in Western Europe! If you had ever asked me back home if such violence could ever happen to me, I would have denied it. Life is full of surprises!

He took the ticket without a word and left the flat, only to come back the following day early in the morning. To make matters worse, it was a cold early May morning and rainy. And he expected to sleep undisturbed in the small room where we were all in and you can imagine how strenuous it is for a child to be told not to talk, leave alone play, a child who was used to a violence-free home with a lot of playing space. I had to take my son to the kitchen and lock it to control his movements. You can imagine what was going on in my mind at this time. To make matters worse, the father was snoring, I would have gone out with my son but unfortunately it was wet and cold, not to mention that we had brought only summer clothes from Kenya which were unsuitable for the European spring weather.

In the afternoon I called Gina, a Kenyan I had recently met in the park, and narrated my "ticket ordeal". I needed to share my predicament, otherwise I would have gone bananas! Unfortunately I came to learn years later that almost every Kenyan in Berlin who knew Gina was informed about this saga, including many private discussions I had with her. Then I thought I was confiding in a friend, but unfortunately, for reasons I have failed to understand up to this day, she was too happy to tell other Kenyans that "Tara, the hot reporter from Kenya will now know that this is Berlin and that Germany is no place for educated Africans".

Gina was like an encyclopedia. Though her life was no better and even having lived for a long time in Germany illegally, she boasted of knowing all that was German. She wasted no time in telling Kenyans that there was no future for educated black people in Germany. She could give examples of how some black intellectuals went seeking employment and how the resource personnel turned them down under minor pretexts. Though I might never have the information of who those blacks were, I have now lived long enough in Germany to see practising black doctors, university lecturers, lawyers, journalists, to mention but a few. There is a big Cameroonian student community in Germany too. The numbers might not be many but they exist. Gina herself later worked for a German tour company but later claimed she was sacked on racial grounds. I am not denying that black people are confronted with racism in Germany, more so because of their distinct colour. Don't be surprised when, if you are black, you enter a German bus and people squeeze on seats, leaving the empty chair next to you unoccupied.Dont be surprised if you meet people smiling on the

streets and when they see you their faces change with hate looks. It has happened to me too. Once I attended a church mass in Eastern Berlin, Erkner. People squeezed themselves in their chairs and I sat all alone on a long and empty bench. Later the priest sensed what was going on and, I assume as an apology and out of politeness, he came to talk to me after the mass. I have met cashiers in supermarket who even wanted to show me how to arrange products on the belt, with the assumption that such things are foreign to me as an African! Recently I met a hairdresser near Rathaus Friedenau who assumed that I had never heard of centimetres! You should have seen her make an effort of writing down on paper what a complicated measurement a centimetre is, so that I could keep the paper and bring it to her next time I wanted my son's hair cut! Such things I keep as souvenirs! Sometimes such people are left speechless when I respond in German and criticise their attitude. Those who know me know that I mince no words at such attitudes, the same way I reacted back home to chauvinistic remarks! Their reaction is that of surprise, for in most cases they are rude to Africans and they rarely get a reaction, I'm sure they assume that Africans are timid, but they should know that a lot has to do with the language. Because of living in Germany, I have been confronted with the realisation of the importance of a language. You can be intelligent, but without a people's language you are a lame duck, a very painful experience!
I have watched with concern some television programmes in Germany referring boldly to black actors as Nigger when there is a "quarrel scene", and so there is nothing wrong artistically by using such phrases. Recently I sent a protest letter to one of the television stations for airing a programme labelled "Wie die Wilden". In this TV series they showed how Germans try to live and cope with native tribes in Namibia, Togo and Indonesia. The translation for the word "Wilde" is Savages and I could not bring myself to understand this insensitive production. Whoever they are referring to as savages are noble cultures which have survived colonial suppression and christianity.

These are proud people who are friendly and tolerant, or are the German characters in the programme who snubbed the ways of the natives the savages? In my racist lonesome "war" in Germany I also called the embassies concerned but unfortunately the TV series continued, but at least I feel I did what I had to do. An e-mail I forwarded to complain about the above never saw an answer from the Television station concerned. Last Christmas, all the main newspapers in Germany carried a front-line photo of a smiling Chancellor Angela Merkel and three white children, one of them painted coal-black with a turban, representing one of the biblical wise men from the east who visited Jesus after he was born! The mission of the three children was to emphasize charity in helping poor third world children! The newspaper headlines focused on German chancellor Mrs. Merkel receiving the black-painted child, exclaiming "The chancellor sees black". As a black person I could not see the beauty of a black-painted white child with an Aladin turban, I asked myself why not present a non-white wise man (is it unfathomable?),afterall one of the biblical wisemen was not white. why not take a natural black German child? Did the painted face indicate that the were no black children good enough to visit the head of state? Did the organisers underrate the reaction of the black community in Germany? Interesting to note was also that the occasion was aimed at raising awareness and charity for the world's poor.Is it not motivating or a black german chld to vist the head of state? What is Intergration? These are some of the daily things that happen in this country and the impact and implications are immense. I watch such incidents with concern and wish for a time when the African lobby will be as politically strong as the Jewish unions here. It is not unique to see an American or French Beauty Company in Germany with models of different colors but it is not a surprise, too, to see the same advert one week later minus the black model (remember a highly marketed Body Lotion with several, not the usual slim girls, it was a break from the usually thin models, more so because there was a black girl among the lot.

Regrettably there is no strong African political lobby in Germany. That will take generations, since the majority of Africans here are people with a basic education or none at all, they are manual workers and more interested in their daily survival than in a political lobby. The Neo-Nazi's on the other hand shave their heads clean, wear military regalia including boots, thus resembling the "SS"-army of Adolph Hitler. This is not only in Germany, there are reported similar backlashes against foreigners in various western countries. It is a controversial issue but I blame the politicians who use the issue to suit their interests. Ordinary westerners are made to believe that their "heaven" is being invaded by foreigners, yet immigration happens in almost every country of the world…

Statistics actually show that the poor countries carry the biggest immigration burden, yet the western media never tell their ordinary readers this! The picture they paint is similar to that of locusts (Africans) invading the west, but the truth is that the African migrant population has a very low demographic impact. The truth is, poor as Africa is believed to be, it has its own share of immigrants. Kenya for example in the 80s hosted approximately 220.000 refugees out of which 140.000 were Somalis, 70.000 Sudanese, 10.000 Ethiopians, but only 2.000 Kenyans sought residence outside the country! And compare this figure to the United Kingdom which the press depict as a country being invaded. In 2003 it had 61.000 asylum applicants! History has shown that humanity has always moved for various reasons, be it hunger, wars, the reasons are many. Or is the west forgetting how they moved to Africa or America, I have a feeling that some Europeans want us to pretend that America has always belonged to them, or how do you justify the usage of terminologies like Afro- American and Latino-American yet nobody uses the word Anglo- American or am I missing something here?

It is obvious that nature demands that you don't stay in one place and die of hunger and poverty. We don't have to watch the migration of a million animals from the Serengeti in Tanzania to Maasai Mara in Kenya to understand this! Or come closer to home and think of the many tourists in Italy at summer's end who watch the migrations of millions of birds crossing the Mediterranean Sea to Africa, escaping the acute European winter, wonderful sight and nature's law but, my friend, such beauty is not seen when it comes to humans, refugees trying to escape the woes affecting West and North Africa, fleeing to Europe! By the way, the Kenya and Tanzanian governments don't restrict the animals to the borders the British erected, and the same applies to the Maasai herdsmen who graze their animals and visit their relatives across the borders, ignoring the colonial demarcation which divided them, people who belong to the same country! It is what happened to the Europeans in the 18th century, they moved all over the world. In today's situation they would be called asylum seekers, yet we in Africa and the native Americans accepted them with open hands. We did not harass them they way they do us at their airports, we gave them land, food and we did not even ask them for passports, we made them welcome! What would you do if you lived in the Niger delta region of Nigeria, where western oil companies erect pumps on people's land without compensating the owners? The Nigeria government even passed a federal law in 1978 (the land use act of 1978) which makes the government the owner of land in Nigeria! The Niger delta people feel exploited and betrayed by their own government and western firms and companies who collude with the authorities to rob them. I don't blame them for crowding boats and heading to Western countries to indirectly share the fruits of their stolen wealth! These oil companies know the injustices they are instilling, their governments too could put pressure on them but all are mum! The refugee problem on the coast of southern Europe is put in one basket by the western press. The western media strengthen their stereotype reports about Africa, they never tell the ordinary citizens that only people from a few countries in the north and west of the Sahara with bad governance are migrating to Europe. The greater part of the African continent from Kenya to South Africa has not a single refugee in those boats in the Mediterranean Sea. Yes, the African continent is composed of lands and peoples, not all of whom are involved to the vagaries of war, poor governance, poverty, starvation or other types of catastrophe as the Western media would have the World believe. It talks of people dying of hunger in Ethiopia, yet nobody talks of the still existing colonial treaty, signed by the colonial heavyweight Britain, forbidding the countries where the river Nile goes through to use its water for farming to benefit Egypt! The same superpowers are silently or should I say "generously reciprocating" together with Egypt, by digging salty water boreholes in exchange for the fresh River Nile water for the countries where the river Nile originates, in terms of development assistance!

I feel it is time the western press stopped telling lies about our continent. Before the west came to Africa, we had names for our lakes and mountains which the later claim to have discovered, we had a rich culture and mind you, corruption was not known. We planted and stored our foods, we even used to cook our food or is somebody disputing that too? Yes, we discovered a lot of things which we cherished for humanity and did not sell the patents, some of which they borrowed when they trekked to the north before the Mediterranean divided us! The list is endless - …

The westerners have to admit we have a golden hospitality culture! Or is it a suicidal culture? The other day I was watching a documentary on television about the first reaction of the native Americans when they sighted the first white people in their land, and you know what they did? They rushed to cover them with warm animal skins, for they thought their fair-skinned visitors were sick, what a generosity! Compare it with the pictures we see of scores of asylum seekers kept in ships at the coast of Italy awaiting deportation. Remember the current cry in the west on the issue of land in Zimbabwe? I'm not a supporter of President Mugabe, but I understand the cry of the landless in Zimbabwe who lost their fertile land to white settlers. The western press never even bothered once to show us the plight of the African workers on white farms, their makeshift carton-homes in comparison to the Victorian villas and how much they earn, the only thing they show us on television is the bleeding white settlers. Or do journalism rules of a balanced story change when it comes to African issues? The truth of the matter is that colonial powers grabbed the best land in Africa without paying a penny and pushed the owners into infertile areas, this injustice is echoed all over the continent. The displacement of Africans and loss of ancestral land led to uprisings like the Mau Mau movement in Kenya in the 1950s and saw the end of the British rule in that country. Some countries tried to fairly sort out the problem after independence but it still persists.

The issue of land in Africa should not be seen with western eyes. The west sees land as an economic catalyst, just like bank accounts and stocks, but for Africans this goes beyond monetary value, it is identity, roots, the attachment is immense. When we die, we are not buried in cemeteries, one owns a piece of land where one hopes to be buried later, death is not the end, we believe the dead are among the living. Many communities in Africa do not have the word "death" in their vocabulary. They instead have words like "he has been recalled, gone home, sleeping...", meaning another phase of existence but not extinction. Most religions in Africa and they are as many as the tribes (many people in the west don't know that Africans had religions, just like the way ordinary Germans assume that Africa is one country like Germany. I'm actually amazed when somebody here asks me "do you speak African?" I'm almost tempted to ask back "do you speak European?") poured libations and offered food and animals to the dead, for we believe the dead are among us and are reborn. That's why we give names of the dead to the new born, for the dead continue living! And that is why having a child is more important to us than keeping a dog, for we believe a person who does not have children is forgotten forever, it is actually a curse to be childless. Many Africans encounter a culture shock in Germany when whites engage in small talk and give them compliments for their beautiful black children, but conclusively spoil their friendly conversation by saying "But I have a beautiful dog too". That's an unfathomable abuse to the African culture, we love dogs too, but we would never compare them to our children!

My Kamba tribe has to this day a unique custom whereby a childless woman is allowed to "marry" another woman (popularly known as Iweto) to continue her lineage. I put marry in Italics for it should not be confused with what is here referred to as Lesbianism) for such sexual relations are still foreign and taboos to many Africans, believe me we don't even have a word for it! The purported "wife" is actually treated as a daughter-in-law and the children she bears, or if she had any before, continue the lineage of the childless woman and they refer to her as Mwaitu or grandmother, so important is the continuation of lineage. Childless women in my tribe also encourage their husbands to sire children with the new "daughter –in- law". The institution of marriage is also important, for children are the base of the lineage. A childless marriage is not considered a marriage. It is not a surprise therefore, even in modern Kenya, if a childless woman encourages her husband to marry a second wife to bear him children! Don't even ask about a wife becoming jealous when it comes to such situations. Many young men in modern Kenya today find themselves torn between modernity and tradition, and believe me the tradition prevails. Don't be surprised to see young school leavers under pressure from their parents to marry even before they have secured employment! This cultural conflict between modernity and tradition in most cases doesn't work and results in many problems associated with western culture like divorce, depression and "big headed women". In fact, parents who pressure their son into marriage unconsciously believe they have his interests at heart, namely the siring of future children! But modernity requires education and it is actually a non-melting pot. In some strong traditional families, parents even go further and "acquire" a wife for their school- going teenager son (if he is the only one among daughters), so that he can procreate early enough in case he dies!

A case is told in Ukambani, a community which I belong to, of a politician who failed to capture a parliamentary seat because he buried his son in Nairobi instead of on his ancestral land. To the community this was a sign of irresponsibility and such a person could not be trusted to lead and love his people, so deep is the communal belonging and land plays a major role, its loss is a signal of extinction, the attachment goes beyond economics!

I guess you have read or seen on television the World Bank reports where they claim that most Africans live on less than a dollar a day. Goodness, we lived for centuries comfortably without a dollar. A Maasai herdsman does not need a dollar to survive! Give a Maasai ten dollars, let alone one, and a cow and for sure he will choose the cow. Such organisations need to understand the anthropological needs of the people before they start evaluating their life in form of coins. Can you imagine a situation where a Kenyan comes to Germany without a visa, evicts a Bavarian farmer and possesses his land? Why is it so simple for the west to think that they can do this to Africans? I'm of the opinion that the majority of Africans are united on this issue. No wonder that when Mugabe recently attended a conference in France, not a single African came to demonstrate against him, there were a few whites but the press in the west never told their readers of the absence of black Africans in the demonstrations.

And when it comes to awareness, France is not Germany. There is a big politically educated African elite in France who were capable of joining such a demo! Interesting to note too is the silence on the issue from African statesmen. The West pretends not to see or rather ignores this "soft" handling of Mugabe by African leaders, but they know very well what it signifies! Due to biased press reports, the majority of people in the west do not even accept that the hunger in southern Africa has more to do with climate change than Mugabe snatching the fertile land from the white settlers who feed the ignorant Africans! Is the west telling us that we did not know how to feed ourselves before they came to rescue us! How come Africans existed for centuries without their modern farming methods and massive tobacco plantations? Black Kenyans own farms and are a world force which supply the west with coffee, tea and flowers. So those in the West who claim that the blacks in Zimbabwe cannot sustain their country's agriculture should look for another reason! Such advocates should have heard Mugabe when he recently amused an African leaders meeting in Nairobi by asking them "Tell me which part of England grows tea". Though Mugabe has a score to settle with his former colonial power, the truth hit home that many African raw products are exploited by western countries and their patents were stolen! The same counteraccusation applies to the animals in the Maasai Mara and Serengeti, I'm not underlying the growing population of both animals and people and the conflict therein, but the westerners should know that we kept those resources, they should not depict us as slaughterers and naïve. Who brought the scorn of the ivory trade and skin souvenirs to Africa? Some white hunters were known to even use elephant hoofs as ashtrays! And these are the rescuers of nature! African used ivory for ornaments but they did not go to the forests to kill animals for fun, the way they do it to their foxes here! What about the senseless slaughter of seals to make fur coats for the rich? And what about the cruel bull fights in Spain? No, rewrite your TV documentaries and books, Africans neither kill animals nor shoot elephants as a hobby! All those slaughtered elephant tusks ended up in western Villas and believe me, not a single African bought a single tusk. You know the law of supply and demand, somebody in the west asked for the tusks and the Africans provided them, don't misunderstand me but balance your reports, it takes two to...

The same evils are happening to our equatorial forests in Congo and Cameroon, diamond wars... The list is endless and the ordinary westerners think the blame lies solely on the Africans, no, rethink when you wear those diamonds, rethink when you buy massive wooden furniture and at whose expense?
Ordinary westerners don't read hard news and only see Africa as a continent full of woes, wars and poverty. They assume the blame lies on the Africans, partly they are right, for wrong governance and corruption plays a big role in it. But don't forget that an Africa at war benefits arms dealers, a war- torn Zaire is better for illegal diamond peddlers and international timber firms, the list is endless! I am not putting all the blame for the African woes on the west. The truth also is that the majority of the African woes have to do with bad governance. Take a rich country like Nigeria. It is mismanaged and a lot of its citizens are the majority of African immigrants worldwide. If our leaders were efficient, a lot of African problems like poverty and corruption could be eliminated.
Back to my life in Rudow. Things kept on worsening. As summer approached, I kept on spending more time in the park and made a few friends. I also suggested to Kalle that it was time to look for a Kindergarten for our son. To my surprise he said he had no idea of where to start such a procedure and we opted to go to the government office for advice. Come the day and the short-lived parental unison evaporated, all because of a heavy door at the government office! Believe me, on the material day we went to a government house, the Rathaus Neukölln. Those of us who live in Europe know that the majority of such houses are monumental old architecture buildings of massive granites and equipped with mammoth wooden heavy doors. Mind you, a door is about 3 metres high and weighs 50 kilos, so my dear Kalle expected me to open one of the wings of the door for him and when I did not do that, he screamed as usual and left Matata and me in the huge corridors, lost for words. Can a Kenyan back home imagine a mzungu who is not a gentleman, a mzungu who shouts at his girlfriend for not opening a door

for him? Yes, I was my boyfriend's unofficial butler in the 21st century in Western Europe or more so in Germany! It's funny the way our brains work. This incident reminded me of an occasion back in Kenya, where my ex-boyfriend shouted at his driver for not being fast enough in holding the car door for me! In fact, I remember he threatened him with a sack! I wished he saw what was happening to me then, he would have only said, "Tara, is that the mzungu you left me for, pride comes before a fall." Thanks to my strong will, some days later I just walked into a kindergarten (I'd recognised it from the paintings on the building) and secured a place for my son without a hassle and all that without speaking a single german word! I was proud of myself!

Apart from our small and squeezed living quarters, I also suffered from the fact that Kalle had an old washing machine which could not spin-dry the clothes, remember that one couldn't hang clothes outside in the sun as in Africa. What surprised me was that such a machine existed in what in Africa we believed was the modern Europe! To make the matter worse, the wet clothes used to drip in the small living place, leaving it all wet when Kalle took them out on the balcony. I think Kalle was ashamed of this scenario and I was surprised that some days later he bought a modern washing machine with a spin-dryer without a complaint. As usual, a drama always followed! Kalle was so excited about this new achievement that he went as far as taking photos of the new washing machine! I just watched the whole scenario and wondered whether I was dreaming! Such a queer behaviour kept on reminding me how low I had fallen socially! Much as I tried to ignore Kalle's behaviour, reality kept on beckoning! In addition, he called his batch of friends and his mother and narrated proudly of his new purchase and achievement! Once more I silently asked myself what I had gotten myself into! My son at this time too requested me to buy him a bicycle, for I hadn't wanted to bring his bicycle from Kenya to Germany. As it is normal, I requested the father to grant his wish, after all here he was having almost a

four-year- old son whom he had never given a present. To my amazement Kalle yelled at me and told me as usual that he was not a millionaire. By this time I hated the man more than I could imagine. I quietly told him that he could take some of my gold rings and sell them for the purchase of the bicycle, and believe me, I meant it, a suggestion he jumped to. Up to this day I have never forgiven him for selling cheaply one of my expensive rings with a tanzanite stone.
A day later, after selling two of my many gold rings (I collect gold with obsession,) he came home with five hundred marks. The following day I bought my son the much requested bicycle. To my surprise the same day I bought the bike, Kalle came home and announced that he had bought a car for me since "you have always thought you were a princess". My God, how do you analyse such a character? Here was a man who categorically refused to buy a bicycle for 350 Marks for his son, claiming that he had no money, and on the same day buys a second hand car for 10.000 Deutsch Marks. What the hell had I gotten myself into? Was I living unknowingly with a psychopant? From then on I vowed to look for a solution to my problems before it was too late. Because of his uncaring attitude, I at one time out of anger told him that I intended to look for adoptive parents for my son in Germany. The answer I got I have never forgotten to this day. He coldly looked at me and said, "Forget it, children with such a skin color have no chance of an adoption in the German society!"
I was flabbergasted. How come he had a relationship with a woman who has a darker color than his mixed offspring? Was this man a racist? Was he with me because he had no chance of getting a German woman? And if so, how did he reconcile it with his feelings? Worse still, one day I saw a dark haired woman on television reading the news, her name was Katja. For me, the name was semantically similar to Khadija. Innocently I asked Kalle whether that was a German name and got this answer: "What do you think, Turkish? Forget it, there are no foreigners on German television." Besides the racist undertone, I

only realised that this man was trying to discourage me in every way possible from going back to my career and believe me, strong as I thought I was, it took me a lot of courage to start afresh. They say it takes a strong will to do so. I also came to know that the claim of only blond-haired broadcasters was just a racial remark and an inferiority complex, or did he mean not to know famous broadcasters born of African parents, like Cherno Jobatey or Arabella Kiesbauer, not to mention scores of the Jewish and Turkish elite! Or did he want to bury his head in the sand and run away from his inferiority complex?

When I later met groups of Kenyans ridiculing their German husbands for paying expensive language schools for them which they were proud to say they secretly deserted after the first lessons, for lack of interest, I only wondered why the world was so unfair, here I was, stranded, not knowing where to begin, no motivation from my friend, yet some people had the chance, but threw the opportunity through the window. Such Kenyans claimed that their men were stupid, for they did not understand their priorities, claiming that they came to Germany to earn money and not to learn. To remain sane, I kept on reminding myself of a line in Desiderata which says, "Don't compare yourself to others, otherwise you will be bitter." I felt so lost and helpless, you can't imagine what's it like, after having been in charge of your own life to be reduced to a level where, if you wanted to write a letter, you had to dictate it to somebody. Remember the illiterate Kenyan village women with husbands working in towns and who seek help from literate neighbours to write a letter? It is a horrible feeling, believe me, which I never wish anybody of my level to experience! One is robbed of one's self-esteem and identity. It is a similar problem facing educated Kenyans brought to Germany by illiterate relatives living here. The illiterate Safari partners have an easier time adjusting. Their goal was to come to Europe (ulaya), period. Unfortunately their educated relatives have dreams beyond Ulaya and "Safari partners" and are confronted with immigrant legalities procedures, a new language and a basis to build their life on. In most cases they are not equipped with the necessary information for such situations. Instead they are promised a life in paradise, a lot of cultural bias and lack of information. One is robbed of one's identity. It is like a replica of what the colonialists did to Africa. Changed our culture and names. They even changed the names of lakes like Nyasa to Lake Victoria, Lake Turkna to Lake Rudolf, ever read history books about Kenya where they write that the first man to see Mt. Kilimanjaro was...? It is as if the Chagga community, who inhabit Mt. Kilimanjaro environs and have conserved it for centuries and for whom Kilimanjaro was their Holy Mountain, weren't humans, compared to this European explorer! Wherever Europe went, it changed the territories. Some of the biggest world problems we have today can be traced back to that redrawing and renaming.

As a reporter, I covered the ethnic clashes in Ruanda and what I saw there is beyond words. When you imagine that such a problem was initially created by the colonialists, it is unforgivable. We had no superior tribes in Africa. Then came the colonialists to Rwanda and chose the tall, European-looking Tutsis to be the masters of the generally "African"-looking Hutus. They gave one tribe formal education and excluded the other. The future differences were institutionalised and the seeds of bitterness were planted, but ask the majority of the Westerners today, they will tell you that civil strife is an African problem! It is not true. Maybe we should tell the story like this: "Once upon a time, in Africa there were no ethnic massacres, no debts, no guns, no slums, no joblessness, no superior tribes, there were gazelles and not Thomson-Gazelles, there were crocodiles but not only Nile crocodiles, we had our names, then we became Peter, Theresa… Then came the colonialists to develop and civilize the continent. Today we are so civilized that we can put a grenade and a Kalashnikov in use!"

Remember, the European Union is composed of 27 tribes. One small country like Kenya has 42 and we live and trade in peace… Yes, besides our 42 religions and beliefs we have synagogues, mosques and Hindu temples side by side. Any religion can buy land anywhere in Kenya and no native Kenyan will raise a finger against it, we not only have religious freedom on paper, but in practice. I cannot understand why some politicians here have something against a mosque being built in Berlin. In a Nairobi classroom, the students are a cocktail of nationalities and religions, so too are their teachers... Back home we are told that there is a high level of democracy in western Europe, but when I see such discussions I am at a loss with words. In Kenyan schools we have Muslim children with scarfs, Maasai children in their raps, Indian Sikhs with their turbans and African "rebels in minis", but we listen to our black, brown and white teachers without problems. We celebrate Bar Mitzvah, Ramadan and Christmas together and harmoniously. Trust me. the Europeans can borrow a leaf of peace from Africa too. Not the whole continent is at war and I doubt whether, there is an African country that produces warfare weapons! Yes rewrite your literature about the old continent.

Then there was the day I bought my son a pair of trousers from the C&A department store. You should have seen Kalles eyes when he saw the paper bag with the logo of the store. He shouted at me and told me to make sure I washed my hands immediately before I came to his apartment, for such a shop was flocked by dirty Turkish people and foreigners. I could not take his racist remarks anymore and told him to go to hell and never to forget that I was a foreigner, period!

In my one-month stay in Neukölln I had also made the acquaintance of an old lady neighbour, Frau Vogel, who spoke English. You cannot imagine how much a difference a language makes. Here was an old lady speaking to me in a language I could understand. That was meaningful, since for us Africans an elderly person is taken with respect. Call it old people's wisdom, but somehow this woman had noticed how unhappy I was. She invited me to her flat which was in the same building, an offer that I was too willing to take. Frau Vogel later turned out to be very helpful, she had a way of letting me pour out my problems and I told her what I and my son were going through. She only remarked "it is always the same story".

I later came to learn that she had helped a lot of foreign women going through what I was experiencing. She gave me an address of an organisation called Frauenzimmer e.V. which was helping women in distress. I immediately called the organisation and was given an appointment. She also gave me a radio station address, "Multi Kulti", where I could look for a job. At first I was surprised, for here was a German telling me to go and look for a job at a radio station, yet the father of my child felt that foreigners had no business in German white collar jobs. Now that I'm informed, the reaction of this man can only be described as that of an ordinary German who feels threatened by foreigners. Such people are insecure, for they don't have careers and they know that they face competition from foreigners in their manual jobs. What is interesting is that somehow they have managed to intimidate some foreigners to an extent that the latter have accepted their creed. One time Kalle came home and told me that he had met an African at our nearby shopping centre. With my always "big mouth" I did not hesitate to ask him what the African did and he said, "What else can an African do in Germany but a manual job in the construction industry!" Now that I live here, I know the reasons why ordinary Germans think like Kalle. Many foreigners come from poor families, coming here was a step towards success, they have a chance to get assistance and attend a language school, even learn how to read and write but this is not as easy as it sounds. They might be willing to, but the pressures back home from their extended families keep them in a vicious circle of poverty. Instead of learning the German language, later a profession and getting a better employment to prove otherwise to the likes of Kalle who think that foreigners can only do manual jobs, they are forced by the circumstances to remain in such a fate. Worse still, before they can stabilise, they are under pressure to bring their wives from Africa, then come the children and the expenses and our African warriors continue their unskilled labour,

come home late and tired to their jobless housewives. The money they earn as cleaners, construction workers or waiters is not enough for the family, let alone financing a language school. Children born of such families in most cases have German language problems, hence poor performance at school and less chances of joining the middle level job market. Kalles list of discouragement and intimidation without looking at the underlying barriers facing foreigners in Germany was enough to break a strong will, but I'm happy, I never caved in!
So too I wish for the black and colored young generation in this country, you don't know how proud I am when I see the first generation of immigrant children in white collar jobs. I hope that with time they will also erase the myth here that black people can only sing and play football. Although these activities are important, it is vital to have a mixture of role models. Africans are not only muscles and music. I dream of a day in Germany when Africans will not appear on screens because of their successful German spouses or music and sport, I dream of a day when an African offspring will sit in a German parliament as an elected Afro-German, I dream of that time when afro issues will be represented in bigger forums, like Jewish issues. I know it is not easy considering the kind of backgrounds our children have, the majority are live in homes where values of education are not known, let alone imparted, they have to do their homework with parents the majority of whom don't speak German and haven't been to school.
Most of them live in cheap residential and crime- infested areas where the temptation is very high to join a gang. The situation is not easy but they shall overcome.
I must mention here too that sometimes when Kalle screamed at me, he could leave small notes in the kitchen on the floor, a behaviour I found puzzling. I asked myself time and time again why this man could not engage in a conversation, why leave me notes?

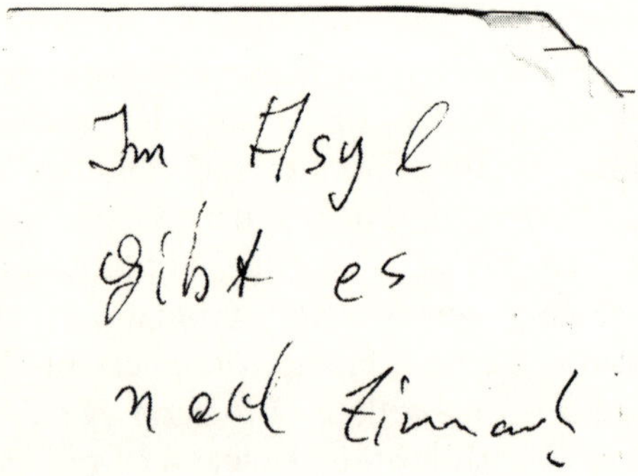

Im Asyl
gibt es
noch Zimmer!

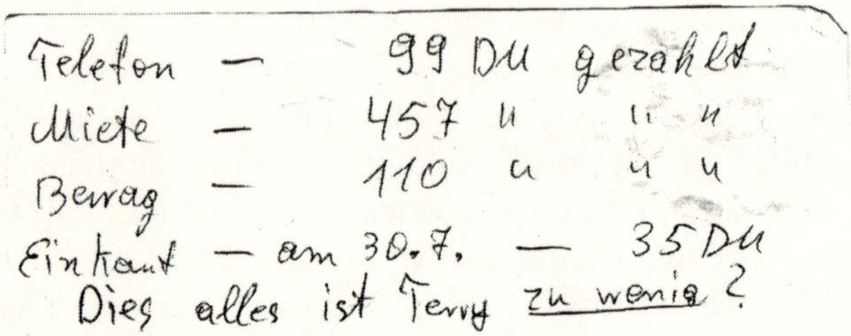

Telefon	—		99 DM	gezahlt	
Miete	—		457 "	"	"
Beitrag	—		110 "	"	"
Einkauf	— am 30.7.	—	35 DM		

Dies alles ist Terry zu wenig?

Some of the notes Kalle placed in his apartment for me since we were not talking, remember I could not speak or write German. The first note translates that I can as well leave and live in a refugee camp! The other two are lists of expenditure in his apartment and that besides being extravagant I was also an ungrateful!

But now I know why. I remember that my university professor, one Odegi Awuondo, said, that people with less intellect tend to engage in aggression, for they have no ability to engage in an argument or conversation. In one of the letters Kalle said: “Im Asyl gibt es ein Zimmer”. I later came to learn that it meant I could as well go to the asylum homes if I was not happy with him. And for sure, any alternative from his one-room-flat loaded with his choleric behaviour was welcome. Frauenhaus, here I come!

LIFE IN THE FRAUENHAUS

I moved in the above on August 27th, 1997. Unlike usual notions and the unhappiness associated with such a the house, I think I was the happiest woman in that house of distress. The two social workers Angelika and Karen asked me whether I wanted to go back to Kenya or stay in Germany. I must mention here that at this time I already had a three year visa which was a topic of discussion amongst Gina's circle of friends. This is so because the majority of them only got visas though marriage. The biggest problem among many Kenyans in Germany is ignorance and the language barrier, they don't seek information and they rely on rumour mongers or German "experts" like Gina. I got my visa on clear-laid German law provisions, which I will explain later. Going to Kenya was for me out of the question. for I had resigned my job voluntarily. I worked in a television station that, unlike today, then had the monopoly of the broadcasting media due to government restrictions. Going back was impossible. The other alternative was to stay, yet I had heard from the "Kenyan experts" in Germany that unless you are married, you could not live here.

However, the two ladies told me that since I was a single mother to a German child, I had the legal right to live here. The Foreign Law in Germany states that every child born of one German parent is by law a German citizen, in other words, German citizenship through birth. Being a single mother, I had the sole custody of my child. What a relief!

Being in the Frauenhaus was for me a break from Kalle's yelling. For the first time since I had arrived in Berlin, I had a place I could call my own, a double-decker bed for me and my son!

The Frauenhaus itself was not a house, but a four-bedroom apartment. The organisation rented such quarters to make the women feel at home despite their problems. It is really a noble work and cause which has helped many women going through all sorts of domestic problems.

I met women who had left home because of violence from their spouses, daughters of muslim parents who could not stand the pressure from their immigrant conservative mothers to marry, and I also met one Heidi Wolf who had left her home on arrival from a Kenyan Safari only to find that her already aggressive teenage son had sold everything in her apartment! Problems affecting women from all walks of life and they were lucky to live in Germany where organisations and individuals financed such institutions and the police too kept their anonymity like a guarded secret.

In the Frauenhaus too I experienced my first winter season in Germany. It was a nightmare. Words cannot explain the degree of coldness to somebody coming from the tropics. In Nairobi and the Kenyan highlands, where tea is grown, the temperatures fall to 9 degrees in June and July but that was far more than minus 3! At that time Kenyans wear jackets and pullovers, but it's nothing near to what I experienced here. One early December morning I decided to go and buy fresh buns for breakfast. The sun was shining and there was a clear blue sky. Judging from my country's weather patterns, I unknowingly assumed that it was warm outside. I was in for a big surprise! The moment I stepped outside, my eyes started flowing, my fingers froze and I felt a sharp pain in my fingers. I had never exprienced such a cruel climate. Breathing, too, became a problem. When I tried to walk to the bakery, I fell down like a sack! It was at that moment that I realised that the ground was slippery. Surprised, too, I noticed that the tarmac looked like glass. Luckily a passer-by helped me up from the ground and explained to me that that one had to wear special boots with a special sole that helped one to stay stable on the ground. The city services too strewed special salts to help the situation. When I came back into the apartment, I wept uncontrollably, I felt so alone and so lost.

Whenever I remember such situations today, I cannot help but laugh at the shocks that await people from the tropics in Europe! Later I was also surprised to watch children slide and play on frozen streams, you could confuse them with the biblical story of Jesus walking on water! Words cannot explain to my countrymen how a stream can freeze and harden like a stone due to coldness, mind you, we can only see snow on Mt. Kenya and Kilimanjaro. Tradition did not allow East Africans to climb and touch snow on the mountains, for it was holy ground. What I experienced in my first winter in Germany can only be explained and equated to putting one's hand in a freezer. This experience erased my schoolday fantasy of snow and winter in geography text books. African school children adore and are bewildered by the beauty of the snow- capped Alps and their environs. The white snow to many in their minds bring the image of a land coated with sugar! I was rudely awaken from this fantasy!

My life is usually full of I would say mystic coincidences. There are lot of things that have happened to me since my childhood that I cannot explain. In elementary school, precisely class two, I used to talk of being a broadcaster, I ended working up there. In High School we had some European volunteer workers and I pictured visiting Germany as a broadcaster, it happened! Coincidentally, my bed in the Frauenhaus was next to a window facing one of the biggest newspaper newsrooms in Germany. Night after night I watched reporters from the window. It was both happiness and sadness for me. Here I was looking at people doing what I used to do, and their action seemed so far away from my life as if that part of me had never existed. Something too happened to me in spring that year. I was visiting a friend in Munich and decided to visit the Versace boutique in the Bayerisch Hof Hotel. Looking at wares, a fellow customer engaged me in small talk. Seconds later, I realised who he was. The man was one of those famous journalists in this country. As if to remind me of my past, I remembered this was a reporter Kalle used to watch with adoration every week, and bewilderment because of his tact with his political interviews. Believe me, sounds infantile but like a small child I later wished that Kalle had been there to see one of his German heroes talking to a foreigner! Me! Up to now, we are good friends…

I have always laughed silently when I imagined starting a home for abused women in Kenya. And woe unto you if you formed one, some male politicians would call you all sorts of names, not to mention the husbands, and I guess you'd be lucky if such a building was not set on fire by the spouses who would give you all sorts of names, "white man's slave", a "frustrated woman", a "prostitute" and "a home-breaker", and worse still, if you started such a noble cause and you were not married. I must mention here that a woman's worth in a vast region in Kenya is measured by the association to a man through marriage and stronger if she has sons, so up to this day a lot of women in Africa with noble ideas, even interest in politics, are put down if they are not married! Yet, we have male politicians who are single or divorced, but the latter unlike the women are not questioned. Remember the recent European Union committee on family issues which was immaturely dissolved after a conservative Italian committee member undermined the role of single mothers? The EU later appointed a new gender-sensitive committee. Such high level unity against gender bias is still a dream for many Africans. The donor countries who give money in the name of Aid should reconsider their strategies, unintentionally half of the aid ends up in men's pockets who are the rulers, thus marginalising the women even more. I am of the opinion that as long as half of the population of the continent is oppressed and marginalised and I'm talking of women, no amount of financial aid will help the Africans. So if you thought malaria, hunger and tribal wars were the main problems in Africa, rethink your strategy! Call me a feminist if you like, but I'm writing about a life I have experienced as a daughter, woman, woman reporter (one time I could not do my story, for a male cameraman refused to take instructions from me, for he thought I as a woman was too imposing on him). Gender imbalance is the biggest cause for poverty and Aids in Africa. As long as women have no say in their relationships with men in fear of losing their daily bread, men will always define their destiny. I know it sounds unbelievable for Europeans, but there are millions of African women who cannot take a family planning pill without permission from their husbands. Such women dare not open their mouths and tell a husband to use a condom, even when he has infected her severely with venereal diseases. You know, the society has been structured like that for many years to make women dependent on men. It is sad that even the ruling elite enjoy legal loopholes, otherwise how do you explain situations where a politician, lawyer by profession, today in Kenya marries the first wife in church, the second in a mosque and many more by traditional customary law, yet such a man can be appointed to head the gender ministry! Why can't Kenya have one official line on marriage? Civil marriage, period! The same men who claim to help women are the same men who exploit the legal loopholes. And don't tell me about African traditions, for such men purport to be traditionalists only when they need something to suit their interests. I know that Kenya as a country as one of the developed countries in Africa can be said to be doing well, but that is not an excuse for more mistakes. Kenyan women have done well both at home and abroad, and we are proud to have the first female Nobel Prize winner in Africa, Professor Wangari Mathai, but still more needs to be done. Prof. Wangari Mathai herself experienced a lot of victimization, not from people who wanted to fell forests on Mount Kenya, but the then government, dominated by men who thought her strong will power was a threat to their authority. Besides locking her in prison to put her down, one afternoon I, then a student, witnessed the demolition by bulldozers of her Green Belt movement offices near the University. The scattered wooden green structures which I knew very well still remain afresh in my mind. A man who impregnates school-going children has it easier campaigning for a parliamentary seat than a single or divorced woman, and don't forget the majority of voters in Kenya are women! The submissive doctrine has run deep in the veins for generations!

An immoral man or a Casanova is still considered a hero!
I stayed in the Frauenhaus from August 1997 to May 1998, when I got my apartment in Berlin-Friedenau. Actually I was sad to leave what had become my home, but I was also looking forward to start a new life. I wanted to learn German and integrate in the country, I wanted to make it my second home, the country of my son.

I started learning the language through the assistance of the welfare office who were also paying for my rent and upkeep.
Summer 1998 I met Tina who, you can say, introduced me to the Berlin "life". They say life is like a theatre. I have heard about both very amusing and sad experiences in these relationships. Tina once narrated to me how a Kenyan lady brought a small village in German to a standstill. The story goes like this:
"Her new mother-in-law gave her a dining table. Her husband did not have immediate transport and she could not wait to furnish her new house. She picked a rope and decided to carry the two metre table on her back, the way she used to fetch water in her Kitui village. She took the matter in her own hands. She used the only road in the village to transport the table. She did not know then that pedestrians have special pavement, colored pink. To her, a road was for everybody, cars, animals and people. She just walked in the middle of the road with the 2-metre table on her back, and a chain of cars at snails speed in her tow! A picturesque site! Those who think that Germans have no patience would have been proved wrong on this day. All the motorists waited patiently until our lady reached her home!" You would have been forgiven to imagine that somebody was shooting a film in the village!
Tina wasted no time in telling me that there was no need of learning German. She stressed that it was easy to learn the language from the streets! Knowing that Tina now has lived more than 20 years in Germany, I can only shake my head at this kind of advice. She, like many other immigrants, speaks only broken German. After learning the language, I realised that Tina could

not differentiate feminine and masculine pronouns. Sadly, she referred to Marco, her son, with a feminine pronoun, I quote: “My son, she is a beautiful boy”, and this is a person who claimed then she could speak German.
Tina’s example is a common phenomenon among many immigrants and it does not make life easier, neither for the immigrants nor the Germans. Tina also kept on discouraging Lulu, one of our girlfriends from the coastal town of Mombasa, that she had no chance of securing a formal employment in Germany. Lulu was new in Germany like me and back in Mombasa she had worked as a secretary. Tina advised Lulu to work as a prostitute, claiming that prostitutes in Germany earned exorbitant amounts that were only a dream for German academics. I could not believe what I was hearing! I come from a country where prostitution is illegal. Unlike in1 Kenya, prostitution is legal in Germany. Tina went on to explain that unlike Kenya, where police harassed and arrested prostitutes, in Germany everybody was equal before the law. At the time Lulu was desperate and decided to take up Tina’s advice however extreme it sounded. Back home her mother was dying of Aids and she could not imagine her mother dying without her. True to Tina’s words, she made money she could only dream of back home. Unfortunately her mother passed away before she could visit, but she had the means to attend the funeral. Later in my apartment I digested what Tina had told us and with that what my countrymen refer to as my rebel mind, I wondered why in my country this trade was not legal, yet women kept on being raped on a daily basis. Or was it time to move the Vatican to Kenya? A lot of hypocrisy in my beloved country! And remember, over 800 people in Kenya die daily of Aids! A catholic bishop even one time burned condoms in Nairobi to emphasize their evil ways. In my country police round up prostitutes, but not the male customers! What Tina said here came to be true to Lulu, and that means she was left with no alternative if she wanted to help her dying mother but to go and work in a sex-club. Judge

her as you like, but to this day she thinks she had to do what she did and her conscience is clear.

The brothel, where Lulu worked was owned by a lady who she later came to learn was a graduate. She only appeared to collect a 3.000 Dollar monthly rent from the Thai woman who was operating it. To Lulu this was a surprise. Prostitution in Kenya was a domain of the poor and uneducated. Here she met people who even had other jobs, but little income and did what they did to supplement their earnings. Students who were addicted to expensive lifestyles, single mothers and even married immigrants who needed money to support their extended families back home.

Here Lulu met people with very interesting stories to tell, the majority of whom were from Thailand. They had married German tourists in cities like Bangkok, Phuket or Pattaya and who had brought them directly from the airport to German sex-clubs. They had to pay for their husband's upkeep, the majority of whom were jobless and received social welfare allowances. For such men bringing foreign girls into the sex trade in Germany was a booming business.

As an African, this was for Lulu stranger than fiction, she could not imagine how an African husband would claim to love a wife and still bring her to work in a brothel. Worse still, the so-called husbands of the Thai women used to sit and wait for their wives when they had a customer in one of the club rooms!

Then there was Carla from Mozambique, Lulu narrated. Carla came to the former East Germany as a child refugee, since there had been war in her country. She did not talk much, and up to this day Lulu says she'll never know why, despite all the German education Carla got, she ended up in prostitution. In November the same year Lulu's mother died and so did her new-founded career. She travelled to Mombasa, Kenya, to bury her beloved mother. For the first time as a grown-up she experienced a loss, and, believe me, there is no grief heavier than death. She earned enough money in the time she was in the club

to clear her mother's hospital bill of 1.2 million Kenyan Shillings without outside help.
I have listened to so many similar stories like Lulu's, and, believe me, I learned a lot from these narrations. I realised that there is so much we take for granted in normal life, we can lose all we have worked for in a day, and life can change drastically. I learned that not all normal-looking people are normal. In Lulu's nightlife narrations I heard things that the three years of sociology I studied at the University of Nairobi, with professors Mbula Bahemuka and Odeki Awuodo, could not have exposed me to. Take for example a well-dressed advocate who comes to a sexual worker, pays for two hours which costs four hundred Euros (40,000 shillings) and wants you to step on his leather jacket for these two hours, he looks at you while doing it, masturbates and then comes!
How about an eighty-year-old man who brings with him a baby doll to the club, pays you for an hour and expects you to wear the sharpest high shoes and requests you to step on the baby-doll eyes for more than an hour!
How about a young college student who pays you and the only thing he wants is to drink your urine!
How about a company executive who books in advance and pays you 1.000 Euro (almost 100,000 Kenyan shillings) to carry home your one-week unwashed pants and a middle-aged doctor who wants you to beat him with a whip until he crawls and that is the only time he gets an erection? Then there is the customer who calls the club to be visited in his house, he pays double the amount and what he requires is faeces on a plate, eats half of it and keeps the rest in his fridge to partake it later! The list is bizarre and endless.
I have always wondered why the West ignore some of the African potentials, I'm saying this because I think there is a lot that could benefit the west without having to have to labour in laboratories and do expensive research. Judging from my experience and other Africans living in the west, the truth is that Africans have a very strong sexual potential. Don't misunderstand

me, I'm not trying to blow the whistle, but the majority of African men have a sexual strength that is comparable to none. The girls I interviewed told me that it can take years to meet a man in the west who can naturally, without Viagra, last 30 minutes in bed, and that is after spending hours trying to arouse him with all sorts of gadgets. Interesting to note too is that the majority of sex workers I talked to told me that one can earn exorbitant sums without having to sleep with a single client. An African man does not need fruits to be placed on his body to be aroused nor does he need to see a woman wearing sexy underwear, believe it or not, an African man does not need to be "blown" to go on heat. Some years back there were press reports in Germany according to which a member of a German aristocratic family, Princess Gloria von Thurn und Taxis (she has investment on the Kenyan Coast), was forced to apologise after she said that Africans were dying of Aids because they like sex! I wondered why the issue was so hotly received and why was it wrong to say what she did? The truth is, Gloria has spent time in Africa and is a known visitor in Kenya, and she can't have created her remarks from thin air! In a way, I was offended to see such a reaction on the African sexual capability. I wished there were such reactions when artists openly refer to black people on the German television as niggers! The truth is, our people have a lot of potential and they utilise it. Princess Gloria should have told her critics that Aids is caused by unprotected sex and poverty. Many Africans to this day avoid protected sex for the mere belief that suggesting the use of a condom to a partner suggests mistrust, not to mention the influence of the Catholic church, too, and its stand on condoms. In my country 800 people die daily of AIDS, yet a catholic bishop has the courage to burn condoms demonstratively to forbid their use! Poverty too plays a great role, many people engage in sex to get a free way to employment, favours of all sorts and remember, the majority of people with resources are men, men who live in polygamous relationships, men who believe that a woman's opinion is irrelevant, men who inherit property in-

stead of children of both sexes, men who inherit by force widows of their brothers who died of Aids due to traditional requirements, the causes are many and complex and the sexual potential of the men still complicates it all, so I wish I could bail out our poor princess Gloria!
In summary, the Aids epidemic in Africa has more to do with attitude, gender imbalance and poverty! And don't believe the chimpanzee theory that Aids originated in Africa, we lived with those lovely animals for centuries. What I don't know is where Africans get their sexual potency from, my layman point of view is that the African sexual potencial has a lot do with the climate and the food we consume and the sun! This seems to be confirmed by a recently published study in a German newspaper, that one does not need t take viagra. For a good potency a man needs Coco, pineapple and nuts, and those are actually the basic foods in Africa! Believe me, there are millions of men in africa ho do not know what a blow job is! So too are there men and women who cannot even imagine what a man's tongue has to do in a woman's zone. So, white women who marry our black village men, don't be surprised if he gets disgusted at such wishes, don't blame him, for where he comes from such things are not known. Besides pleasure and procreation, sex is a dirty act and so too are the female parts. The "city " Africans surely know such things, but the majority of the men who are in Germany come from villages and low income city states and, let alone a blow job, kissing was never an African tradition! Neither is Orgasm for an African woman! Millions of African women do not know what an orgasm is, this has to do with traditions that put women as a secondary being, her pleasure is not a priority, sex is made to please the man and to make children, so what a woman feels in bed is irrelevant. The majority of men in Africa don't arouse their women, they just climb on her, "pump" her, and the act is over when the man comes. Besides these attitudes, African tradition went further to suppress women's desire by cutting their clitoris: clitoridectomy, a practise which, though illegal, is still practised in the nomadic tribes

of East Africa. Besides denying women the pleasure of sex, such practises cause death in childhood and also in childbirth. The Kenyan government has gone further to educate nomads on stopping the practise and retain girls in schools during circumcision seasons, but you will be surprised actually because resistance to stop clitoridectomy comes more from the women than the men. Some girls escape from their boarding schools to voluntarily undergo the rite! This is because the majority of women through the years have come to value the practise, believing that a woman is only fully a woman and respected in society if she is circumcised!

Time and time again I asked myself why. Why do the Europeans have such a variety of sexual behaviours, was this civilisation? Was this what the Africans craved for? Was this what the Africans were heading to? Did this have to do with the weather, the food or democratization? What was wrong in this society or was it me who was primitive and conservative? Why do western men sexually abuse and kill children? Could the reason be that they prefer thin and girl-like looking women? Sometimes when I see such reports, I realise the gift of freedom that children in Africa have, they play in the fields without the supervision of parents watching them in fear of sex molesters, they trust almost all grown-up people, for anybody the age of parents is respected in Africa. One of the first culture shocks Africans experience when they see parents here acompanying children to playgrounds, reminds me of the way some animals guard their prey from the vultures! Initially one can be excused to think that such parents are idle or paranoid. The truth is, child sex molesters have been known to snatch children from playgrounds or even molested and killed children in such areas. Much as I tried to analyse Lulu's narrations, I have never found answers or the missing links between the two continents. After Lulu's mothers burial she never went back to Berlin's nightlife. She registered in the famous Hartnack-Schule for German lessons. After a six months' spell she looked for a job and got one in a library.

And as I'm writing this book, I'm thinking about what I have gone through in Germany, my childhood, schooldays, university life and life as a reporter back home.
So much happens in a lifetime. The little village-girl I used to be, looking after cattle, passing well to go to Tumu Tumu High School and later to the university Nairobi, to the surprise of many in the village.
I say surprise because those male chauvinistic attitudes did not expect a girl without a father to do well in school.
My primary school days, the discriminations I went through for being "fatherless", yet no child can be born without a father. I must mention here that I am the child of a single mother. In the Kenyan rural areas, children born by single mothers are shunned, for they are perceived to be conceived in sin! One of the christian teachings! Such are the teachings of christianity which replaced African traditions! In my tribe's tradition, all children belonged to the community, virginity was not valued, but all of this was changed by christianity. Such children bear a bulk of discrimination from the society and in school. It is not a surprise if there is a wedding and such a child is not welcome in the "singing group" for the newly weds. Furthermore, such a group must wear new clothes on the wedding day and chances are the poor single mother cannot afford such a luxury. Most single mothers living in rural Kenya are poor. They live like squatters in their parent's homestead and to this day, 90 percent of Kenyan families divide their ancestral land to their sons and leave daughters without any. Can you imagine here your own parents dividing land or property to your younger brothers because they are men, and you being left out even when you have children to feed, what a cruelty! So if you thought that the Islam discriminated women, think twice! The Koran calls for inheritance for both men and women
From the Frauenhaus I have had to learn German and secured a correspondent job as a news reporter with a German radio station. I have gone through hard times in Berlin, but I love this city. From the active television reporter in Kenya I landed in

Germany and my world took an upside turn. I have lived on social welfare, worked in care homes, in bakeries with night shifts until you could not recognise my face covered of flour… I even became a laughing stock to some of my countrymen living here, for they saw the change of my lifestyle as God's way of balancing life between the haves and havenots or is it sadism? In Kiswahili we say "Asiyefunzwa na mamaye hufunzwa na ulimwengu (He who is not taught by her mother is taught by the world)", and believe me, the world has taught me many things in Germany!)

Kalle's behaviour has never changed to this day. He intentionally has an unofficial job (Schwarzarbeit) to avoid paying for his son's upkeep. He even took me to court with an official written support, full of framed accusations from Tina to take my son away. In a copy from Kalle's advocate, Tina fabricated a lie that she could witness that I was not a responsible mother. I understand that for this lie she was bought beers! Fortunately, the family court in Kreuzberg listened to my story and only granted Kalle the right to see the son he only fathered under the supervision of the German Red Cross (Betreuerumgang). The court made this decision since I had argued that his aggressive behaviour was a danger to my son. The whole process was a show and after only 2 visits he abandoned the whole procedure. I have never heard from him to date, no telephone call to his son, not even on his birthdays or Christmas festivities. My son is now 13 years old and his father has never introduced him to his parents. As for Matata, my initial aims have so far been rewarded: he is in one of the prestigious High School in Berlin Zehlendorf. As for me, much has not changed, I have a friend, a German and a surgeon who has no complex with an independent African partner. Financially I'm not rich, but I live in Berlin's noble district Zehlendorf in a historical 100-year-old villa, mind you, my nextdoor neighbour is a renowned controversial German Prince. Back home, one of my former colleagues is now the foreign minister! It is one of those destiny comedies that surround and fulfil my life and I love them unfolding like a

desert flower in the middle of nowhere! In Germany I have lived it all, poverty, social welfare benefits, where I was scorned in the queue by homeless and stinking people who felt I had no business collecting welfare benefits earned by their own. In such situations you learn to be patient and know that you can't yell at everybody and say "Hey chaps, I'm not one of those who want to reap where they did not sow, I went to school, goddammit 16 good years, I had a job until my heart led me to your honey country". You just can't tell everybody and justify your situation, you just let them have their judgement and learn to live with it. Call it dying nobly.
As a correspondent I have met the mighty in this country, too. I have mingled with them and interviewed them, but at the back of my mind such occasions always make me homesick. Call it homesick or a prisoner of one's identity. I have mingled with the mighty at Galas My safari in Germany has been a melting pot of various concoctions and believe it or not, I love it! Safari offspring's and their literate parents, do me a favour and read a book called "Destined to Witness," the story of a colored child in Nazi Germany by Hans Marsquoi.

I take pride in helping people and in Berlin helped many to my detriment. I don't regret helping them. It is rare to receive gratitude from a Kenyan you helped in Germany. Instead, they emphasize anything that might have caused differences between you and them. Unfortunately there is a lot of loose talk, witch hunting and character assassination among our people living in Germany. A German might not understand this, but the cadre of the majority of Kenyans in Germany are what you would describe "from rags to riches", they are not rich in the real sense of the word, but in their world, coming to Germany or Ulaya was like hitting the jackpot! Some of the people are married to lawyers and doctors, something they could only dream of in Kenya, even in Germany it is almost impossible to imagine a doctor married to a semi- illiterate woman, for this group of people that is an ultimate achievement and anybody who challenges their authority is declared persona non grata. It is a big clout with solidarity! I'm sure my book will not amuse some "Safari partners", for it unearthes some of their closely guarded secrets f their Garden of Eden! Or should I say "paradise made in Germany"? But I hope it will help those willing to migrate here to have some basic knowledge of what brews in this "paradise"! I silently smile when I imagine how they will discuss and create stories about this publication, yet they will not bother to read it! Or are they able to read it? For the majority of this group, reading culture is foreign.

I believe a lot of animosity has to do with their backgrounds, frustrations and idleness. It is also a result of broken dreams and high expectations. They have had to cope with the reality that not every white man is rich, like many immigrants, they have seen that one does not collect money on German streets! They cannot accept that they are in Europe and poor, it pains them to the core, and what do you think they will tell their relatives back home? The human ego cannot allow them to accept their fate, their curse of being in Europe (Ulaya) and not rich, for many stranger than fiction. Their social home background did not prepare them to be independent. What is normal for a clerk back in Kenya, like renting an apartment and answering official letters, is not so simple here. So to fill this gap, they have to stay with difficult partners for survival. They move from one partner to the other, they cannot contemplate self - reliance or even dare to, simple things like renting an apartment is like an amateur climbing Mt. Kilimanjaro for them. Here renting an apartments means paperwork, one has to show one's income, police registration, anything needs documents and for Safari partners from Kenya that is a tall order! The majority cannot read and write in German. Without the language there is no job, no money and no apartment, one is incapacitated. It is a similar situation like back home where millions of housewives in Africa have to live with abusive husbands for financial security. But unlike home, one has an alternative here, government-sponsored trainings. Such groups of people release their frustrations in bars, drink and fight and talk of ho is doing what, hard but reality. That's my land of wealth made in Germany! Somehow I don't understand how somebody without primary school education, who had no job in Kenya, expects to miraculously find a white collar job in Germany, not to mention the lack of interest in learning the German language. In Germany there are a lot of opportunities for training at what is called "The Public School – Volkshochschule". The government sponsors courses ranging from alphabet level to catering and music, mention it, even bicycle riding for women immigrants who were not allowed to ride bicycles by their suppressing male societies. The opportunities are immense and the basis is the language which most of our people don't want to learn or are scared of learning, and without it the only alternative is unskilled labour, low ages, joblessness, bitterness and frustration, culminating in heavy drinking! The press in Germany also does not make integration easier. Just like most of the western press, German journalists highlight only what is negative in Africa. Africans here make news when they are attacked by Neo-Nazis or commit a crime. Positive news or a "success" is usually when a black girl befriends a prominent German! Those of you who live in Berlin might remember a newspaper headline with the alliteration "The killer from Kongo", mind you, the said accused was a colored young German man with Kongo heritage and since he committed a crime, he was more Congolese than German! Worse still, when there are issues facing the African continent, the press here then prefer interviewing German "experts" who have spent a week in an African village to an African intellectual who knows the situation hand in and out!

How about a press conference where I was present and where the former Mercedes Benz chairman Jürgen Schrempp had invited several African Presidents, among them King Mswati of Swaziland, among others. Schrempp's intention was to strengthen economic links with South African countries, but my colleagues were more interested in Mswati's many wives and worse still, one of the main television channels here zoomed in on an African leader for almost a minute while he was putting a finger in his nose (it is considered dirty and uncultured in Europe to put a finger in your nose in public)! My opinion is that the African community in Germany is here to stay, and a balanced attitude is needed for a smooth integration. I have done as much as I can to help victims of "Safari partner". I come from a social strata where an intellectual opinion is accepted. My trouble with "Safari partners" was to impart my intellectual opinions. I guess I made a mistake in assuming that they could take criticism on the same level of understanding without feeling intimidated. They were just like Kalle, he knew I was more educated than him and wanted to put me down. I was too much of a Matata (trouble) for his low self-esteem. I was wrong.

I see myself as a wild flower. Like a wildflower, I have decided to uproot myself from the many safari partners and let the wind carry me in writing this book. Like a wild flower, I have had to branch out from the "norm" of silence and tell the story of our "paradise". It will have repercussions, but don't you worry, I will survive. I never belonged, and telling this story was one way of setting the wildflower free! A lot of my countrymen here hate the truth with legendary passion. Call it absence of vision and political myopia! Like the late South African freedom fighter Steve Biko, I write what I like and I like what I write, that is freedom. I don't expect gratitude from them, but only hope that they who like this book will in turn help such victims of "Safari partner" experiences and eradicate the myth of wealth made in Germany! Aluta continua!

BERND

Bernd was born in the renowned mountainous province of Bavaria, Bayern in German. A son of a successful farmer, Bernd went to good schools, later to college where he graduated with a diploma on computer management. Though to many Bernd seemed happy and successful, in his inner self there was a missing link. Like many other country children the city fascinated him, a factor that led him to look for a job in a big city. He needed a city where there was freedom of an individual and any person living in Germany can guess where Bernd landed: Berlin.

In early 1970ies he secured a job in one of Berlin's saving banks. At last he thought he had achieved what he always wanted. In Berlin, with a population of over three million inhabitants, he was just like a grain in a big silo. Unlike in Bayern, the Berliners were impersonal and everybody minded their own business. Unlike in his native province of Bavaria, in Berlin what you did was not your neighbour's business. In Berlin Bernd had a problem of freedom of choice and a variety of entertainments in then West-Berlin. Though there was the shadow of communism and the famous Berlin Wall that divided the city into two, life proved to be normal for the Bayer in Berlin.

In his free time Bernd used to frequent Berlin bars and with no hassle he became a renowned customer in one of the Irish Pubs in the Europa Centre, Ku'damm area. This is located in the then central business district of the western part of the city. Little did he know that in this pub something would happen which would change his entire life forever, call it destiny.

One summer afternoon he was sipping his Berliner Kindl beer and listening to a life band when a young African man walked in and requested to sit next to him. In a short span of time, the two engaged in a conversation that led Bernd to know that the young man, Mutua was his name, was a Kenyan. The stories Mutua narrated about his homeland fascinated Bernd. Not because this was the first time to hear about Kenya, but he was hearing and sharing beer with a very friendly person. He already knew Kenya as a famous tourist destination with beautiful savannah grass lands, animals and famous safaris. Many Hollywood films and books are set in Kenya. Films like *The man-eaters of Tsavo, I Dreamed of Africa, Hatari, Out of Africa, Irgendwo in Africa* etc. Kenya was famous for its long distance runners, too, not to mention the famous archaeological findings of the early man. Come to think of it, Bernd was talking to a close descendant of the early man! Yes, the Kenyan Rift Valley was known for its archaeological findings. What was for Bernd a normal current affairs discussion about the early man, surprisingly seemed to be alien to Mutua. He concentrated more on the topics of holiday issues. And Bernd opted not to bore the young man with his knowledge about current affairs. Here was Mutua telling him about the cultures of the Maasai warriors, polygamy and the many beautiful Kenyan girls who are looking for mzungus (white men) to marry! Oh, that was the catch and Mutua knew the topic, he himself having been a beach boy and homosexual in Mombasa and having come to Germany through a German tourist. Here was Bernd, lonely and successful, just like the famous 700.000 single and lonely Berliners. And here was an interesting young man who suggested that the 35-year-old Bernd could get an 18-year-old beautiful girl and to crown it, even marry her! That was a catch! That night, Bernd never slept. He made the decision the following day to apply for his annual leave and visit this country of beauty and wonders. Within a period of two months, Bernd landed in Mombasa, the harbour city of Kenya. And in a way he felt at home. The smell of salty sea water, the traditional Arab architecture and the humidity, though foreign, made him feel at home. Apart from moving from Bayern to Berlin, Bernd had never been outside Germany. So this was quite a trip.

From Mombasa Airport he boarded a taxi which took him to his hotel in the Bamburi Area of Mombasa. The friendly taxi man already taught him some useful Kiswahili words, like the greeting "jambo", no problem to mean "hakuna matata" and "kuna matiti", meaning "there are only breasts", a play on words, really the typical tourist communication stuff. Bernd was fascinated. He saw poor-looking people, but so friendly, the difference between these people and the solemn unsmiling Berliners was as a strong difference as the wall dividing the city he came from. Within no time he arrived at the then maintained enterprise of Ocean View Beach Hotel. He had an apartment facing the beach, and the coconut trees were swinging with the rhythm of the sea wind. It was just a dream come true. He remembered once, as a college student, how he read a book by a Kenyan writer Kuki Gallman, named "I Dreamed of Africa", and felt like Kuki herself! What a sight!, what a friendly people. Within a week, the magic of Kenyan coast had bewitched Bernd. He also made lunch and air safari trips to the renowned Maasai Mara Game Reserve, to the Tsavo National Park, as big as Belgium, and to the famous Serengeti Park.

A week before his departure to Germany he hired a car and drove on Malindi Road without any specific destination. He might not have had a destination in mind but I think fate and destiny had already decided. After passing the town of Kilifi and its beautiful Bougainvillea Gardens, he arrived at the nicknamed "Italian" town of Malindi. It is nicknamed "Italian" because a lot of its inhabitants are Italians and there is a lot of Italian influence in terms of language and culture. Prominent Italien investors in Malindi include the Formula One boss Flavio Briatore.

Bernd parked his car outside what looked like a shack bar, thatched with coconut leaves (Makuti), and decided to take a cool bottle of the Kenyan beer "Tusker". The beer is named "Tusker" implying the elephant tusks with a reason. The pioneers of the brewing company were two English brothers, one of whom was killed by an elephant, thus giving the name in his memory.

In this bar Bernd saw a few tourists, but a lot of beautiful African women who were looking and giggling at the men. Little did he know that one of these girls was to be his future wife and would change his life forever.

In a matter of minutes, one of the girl's relatively short but with a beautiful gap between her teeth, requested to sit with him. The gentleman he was, Bernd accepted immediately, not to mention that this was the opportunity he had been dreaming of.
She introduced herself as Tina Nduku. She proceeded to tell him she came from one of the famous tribes in Kenya, called Kamba, not that Bernd knew the difference between the tribes. So the notion of the tribes was meaningless to Bernd, he decided to keep the conversation going and asked what the Kamba people are renowned for. Of course, Tina decided to discuss what was relevant to her being there, and narrated in detail how the Kambas were even put in colonial books "as the sex machines of East Africa".
Tina was a prostitute in Malindi, having come there as a housegirl from Kangundo in Machakos. She met girls from her village who introduced her to the nightlife, a life that made her earn money to support her family in the village and her five-year-old son. Within no time, Bernd and Tina were in good spirits and they started even talking over relationship.
Tina asked Bernd whether he was married and to her joy he responded that he was single. She told Bernd about her kind of work in Malindi and in a course of two-hours meeting, Bernd decided to take the Kamba beauty with him to his hotel in Mombasa. Tina herself decided that Bernd should accompany her to her sisters' house to inform her of her abrupt Mombasa trip. What Tina did not tell Bernd was that she had two more children, a two- and one one-year-old from unknown American soldiers. This was normal for many girls in the business, to get children with sailors "accidentally", since then there was no Aids and people were careless. What was funny about Tina is that she had no contact with the fathers of her two colored children, nor knowledge of their names, after all they were products of one-night-stands. She was unlike some of her girlfriends who kept in contact with the fathers of the children, even if not for love, then for financial support, but this was Tina!

When I later asked Tina why she had several children with strangers in such a short spell of time she said: "You've got to understand the situation I was in, I had a child to feed and in the search for food, I ended up getting more children."
I can understand her situation but I'll never understand why she never kept the names of the men for the interest of her sons. I still believe a child has the right to know his father.

Two days in Mombasa, with its swinging coconut trees and pure white sandy beaches, and Bernd was totally in love with Tina. There and then he decided to bring Tina to Berlin. He could not see life without her. His four-bedroom apartment in Berlin-Grunewald was enough for his newly-founded family. The third day after meeting Tina, Bernd proposed to his Kamba beauty, an idea too welcome for Tina in order to run away from the abject poverty she was living in Malindi.
This mzungu while proposing was nervous, in case Tina refused. Little did he know that he was answering her long-time prayer. After all, every girl in her club was praying to get a mzungu who could bring her to Europe. A paradise where, as many call-girls and beach boys believed, people collected money from the streets. Or is it not so? All the Germans who come to Kenya look rich, not only look rich, but they spend their money generously. Not to mention the girls who are married to them. Those living in Kenya drive big cars and lived in big houses with swimming pools, really a dream for many. Not only prostitutes, but also working class women whose salary cannot afford them good living standards, adore good lifestyles. Many ordinary Kenyans don't know that "the-wealth-made-in-Germany-Show" has nothing to do with every German back home, but more with the strength of foreign currency exchange rates. So, really landing a German and a banker for that matter was similar to winning a raffle for Tina! Out of the blue, Tina became a crusader of traditions and told Bernd that they could not go to Germany before getting a blessing from her parents in Kangundo.

A car was hired, and within two days Bernd unknowingly and symbolically embarked on a lifetime safari to Tala, Tina's home village. Before reaching Tala, Bernd was overwhelmed by the Kenyan landscape. From the swaying and singing-like coconuts and ridges of Mazeira to the flat savannah grassland and thorny acacia trees of Ukambani. From Taita Hills he could see the snow-capped Kilimanjaro Mountain, what a beauty! The many apes, zebras, giraffes and gazelles along the Nairobi-Mombasa highway! The sight was bewitching! Nature seemed to agree with his decision and the beauty of the landscape seemed to confirm it! Then came the almost equatorial climate of Kangundo with expansive coffee plantations, the Koma Rock, a monstrous rock, big as a hill, which Tina explained was once a holy place for the villagers before the coming of the whites with their christianity. Fortunately or unfortunately, on this day it rained heavily. As they drove towards Tina's homestead, Bernd saw a different land scenery tha the one from Mombasa. He saw thatched grass huts, a lot of cattle and maize fields. Tina's home was however a bit different from her neighbours. Kangundo being a coffee-growing area, the majority of the villagers had good income and houses. What struck Bernd most was the sign of abject poverty at Tina's homestead.
Though not an expert, Bernd realised that Tina must have come from one of the poorest Kamba families, a factor that drove him closer to her, for he felt obliged to help. At Tina's home there were no cows, no chicken, but one poorly thatched grass hut, it was the only possession the parents had.
On arrival, Bernd met Tina's frail-looking old parents. They were thin and old. He guessed probably in their seventies, but was later shocked to know that they were in their mid-fifties. Poverty and diseases had reduced them to such creatures. He later came to learn that if one had no job in Kenya, there were no social system benefits. So in most cases people had children as a way for their future social security. In this poverty-stricken family Tina was the only breadwinner and hope. In Tina's

homestead there was only one wooden bed but no mattress. So instead Tina and Bernd had to sleep on the dusty floor.
As fate would have it, that first night in an African village turned out to be a nightmare. It was to linger in Bernd's memories for the rest of his life. Never before in his life did he sleep on a dusty floor, in a half-thatched hut, not to mention without a mattress and a blanket. He realised that what many of his country people took for granted, was a luxury. He almost laughed himself silly when he remembered his high-school camping trips and the fun that accompanied them. But this was not a camping trip, this was a people's way of life and it was not funny. To make matters worse, that night rained cats and dogs, the hut leaked and the whole ground was wet, the mosquitoes had their day too. Tina sympathised and in a way was ashamed, but she had no alternative. She only suggested that they could empty the small pools of water with a calabash, "nzele", a traditional bowel. Bernd was a good learner and with no time kept removing the amassing water from the hut. They also got help from bats. For the first time Bernd saw these creatures, which the Berliners visited in the Citadel of Berlin-Spandau, not as unique mammal nature beauties but as helpers of a balanced ecosystem. Flying swiftly and with finesse, they ate the mosquitoes, thus lessening his suffering, something that was new to him. When Tina narrated this story to me years later in a McDonald's restaurant in Hermannplatz, Berlin-Neukölln, I was amazed. My newly experienced opinion on Germans in a way was altered. Here was a man, so patient, I almost thought she was lying, but how could she fabricate such a story, and there and then I decided one time I will write this story which I am doing now.

The following day the sun rose like a golden fire ball, the sky was blue and clear as if it had not rained. Though Bernd had not slept, the weather brought him into good spirits. He also realised that Tina's homestead, unlike the previous day, was full of people, young and old. Small kids were touching and looking at his elegant hired Pajero car with bewilderment. They were also giggling "mzungu", meaning a white man, after all he was the only white-skinned man in the middle of black villagers who had never travelled to a city and seen white people. It was quite a unique sight. Some of the kids cried because of fear, they thought the white man was a ghost because of his color. In the African mythology a ghost is believed to be white, a devil too. Some even thought he was burnt or sick.

Then there was the "dog-toilet drama". In Tina's compound there was no pit toilet as it is in some villages in Kenya. Bernd had to learn to relieve himself in the bush like the rest of Tina's family. In the afternoon he strode to a near-by thicket for a long call, he had all the necessary "skill" information on the process, thanks to Tina, but the unexpected happened. Usually in such homesteads, food for dogs is a luxury, and the animals have to resort into eating faeces from their masters for survival. Usually they develop a sense of knowing when a person is going to relief himself and it is not a rare occurrence in the village to see dogs squatting and waiting to partake such meals from their masters! What Tina forgot was to inform Bernd about the above and you can imagine the shock Bernd got when seeing four strange dogs staring at him in the bush. He reacted on impulse, thinking that the beasts wanted to attack him. You can imagine the free show he gave the villagers when he emerged from the bush, completely naked, holding his underpants in one hand and screaming at the top of his voice! You can also imagine the sight of a naked mzungu in the midst of black villagers screaming! Children covered their eyes, giggling, and grown-ups ran and took cover in the hut and bushes nearby to spare their visitor the shame.

After realising that her man had not been bitten by a snake, for that is what the villagers initially thought, Tina tried to calm him down and explained the purpose of the dogs in such a situation! Much as Bernd was shocked, so too were the villagers, for in the African culture a man is not expected to show fear, unless he is attacked by a dangerous animal, not even to imagine a naked man screaming like a baby in front of women and children! Just as Bernd was shocked by this incident, so too are many Africans in Europe when they see the luxurious treatment given to domestic animals. I must say though I had attended several dog shows in "British Kenya", I sometimes used to laugh myself silly when I saw Dogs supermarkets in Germany, Dogs Hair Salons, dogs carried in expensive baskets and dressed in expensive clothes. My dear countrymen, you should know there are even dog psychologists in Germany! Berlin also now boasts to have the first 5-star dog and cat hotel! There the animals have baby sitters, swimming pools and massage saloons! It is not that we hate our dogs in Africa, but the pomp the white people treat their animals with is amusing and foolish to African eyes. If you are an African visiting Europe, don't be amused to see European dog owners kissing their pets on the mouth, or don't be surprised if your mzungu husband or wife insists that you will all have to share the bed with their Doggi, or don't be offended if your partner says you don't have to have babies since you have a dog! How many times in Berlin have I seen mothers pushing baby prams with screaming children in them and instead of calming the baby, they are busy talking about their dogs and in my eyes paying more attention to the animal than to their child.

Last year there was a story in the press about a family in Brandenburg near Berlin, in which the police rescued children locked in a hut in cold winter, and the parents were drinking joyfully in a warm house with their dogs lying on a carpet! A Canadian neighbour once told me how she was shocked by one of her friends when she expressed her desire and impatience to see her grown- up son leave so that she could acquire two more dogs! I love animals too, but the intensity with which Europeans love pets is to me a natural puzzle. Or is it that we in Africa are less attached to animals because of the competition for survival? For example, I grew up in a village where there were all sorts of animals, it was a daily routine and ritual for the young boys to kill geckos with slings, it was part of growing up. What about children yearning for meat, and they tie dry grass on a long bamboo stick, torch weaver bird nests in the evening, rejoice at the sight of falling burning birds and roast them over the fire. If one is brought up buying meat from the supermarket, one sees this as a cruelty, whereas others see this as a necessity and creativity, and at no time can I think of comparing my childhood to what I see here, computer games etc. The Kenyan village children do not own bears as toys and don't be surprised that when you give them a baby doll, they will scream, for mistaking it as a dead baby! Ordinary children in Kenyan villages find their ways of entertainment, build themselves wheels for playing.

Culture shock, but be prepared. An African woman will doubt the sanity of her German counterpart who has a room full of dolls as a hobby. Neither can an African understand the feeling of an old person in a home cuddling a toy bear in his bed. Just putting a parent in an old people's home is unforgivable and unimaginable for many Africans. Such cultural barriers need to be understood for the partners to understand each other.

Little did Bernd know that by coming to the village, he had also changed Tina's family status. The fact that Tina had brought a mzungu home was enough to transform the villagers lack of respect for the poor family. Tina's last-born brother, Kyalo, was now also bragging that his prostitute sister had found one of the richest owners of a German bank!

That day the good Bernd also decided to help Tina's parents. In a matter of hours, iron sheets and bricks were bought to start the construction of a semi-permanent house. It did not require an effort to get construction labourers, more so when a Mzungu was involved, for they were known to pay well! By four o'clock that afternoon, construction work had already started and in the following day a three-bedroom house stood on Tina's homestead. Not to mention the polished wooden stools and beautiful melamine plates he had bought at the local market. Who said there was no God? Who said miracles never happen? Only two days ago Tina's family had had no house, no chairs and no

beds, and now there was a three-bedroomed red brick house with chairs and beds! What a transformation!
On the third day after the arrival, Tina had a bull slaughtered for the villagers and took the opportunity to say goodbye, since she was leaving for Europe (Ulaya). Though many Kenyans detest prostitution, the villagers' mood softened when they realised how Tina's life changed. After all, which east African does not remember the song "Shilingi yaua, ah tena maua", with money, people with past misdeeds in Africa seem to be transformed into other beings. This does not only apply to prostitutes, but also to politicians. How many carjackers, drug traffickers or corrupt civil servants turned millionaires are now held in high esteem in society.
Reminds me of a work-mate of mine, Mima, who had a prostitute sister-in-law, living in Germany. She once narrated to me how her brother-in-law, a poorly-paid High Court judge, used to race nervously to the airport in Nairobi to pick up the rich prostitute on arrival. After all, she kept the family going, and her daily earning in Germany was the judge's monthly income.
Money changes devils into saints. Don't misunderstand me, I have nothing against prostitutes. After all I consider them as social workers. They don't rob and they earn their money, unlike corrupt politicians. They take and bank their money in Africa, whereas the African politicians loot their economies and bank their money in Europe. And God knows what will happen to our women and children in Europe if there were no prostitution services. The courts would be full with sex offenders and serial killers, were it not for the prostitutes. Kenyan journalists write screaming headlines when police round up prostitutes. And of course my colleagues approve the wonderful police swoop! Mind you, prostitution is illegal in my country. In my beloved country more than 800 die of Aids daily, in my beloved country the press laments with banner headlines about daily rapes, but unfortunately none of my beloved colleagues analyses the situation and the importance of the role of prostitutes in society. None of them gives a solution to the sexual

needs of factory workers whose wives are in rural areas. I assume no-one, including the politicians, dares to suggest that legalising prostitution could to their surprise reduce rape, divorce and Aids. Those partners, men or women who are bored in their matrimony, could go to sexual workers without having to have a relationship with a girlfriend or boyfriend. A girlfriend who might demand more attention, thus interfering with the family. A girlfriend with whom one does not need to use a condom because she can be trusted! The same girl has a secret lover and keeps the married man for financial comfort, when Aids strikes, they all go! But they die a holy death because they did not sleep with a prostitute! And on goes the cat-and-mouse-game! But with a prostitute one takes precaution without the trust issue. What is more interesting is that the developed countries pumping aid for fighting AIDS to Kenya, legalise prostitution in their home countries, yet they don't question the government's wit of illegalising prostitution in a country losing 800 lives a day to Aids! Talk of double standards! I know I'm walking on fire, talking about the untalkable, treading dangerous grounds. Sex discussions are still a taboo number one theme in my country, let me remain the born rebel, but my conscience is clear!

With two days to go, Tina and Bernd proceeded to Mombasa. Up to this point Tina had not revealed that she had two more children. Bernd suggested a month after coming to Germany she could bring her five-year-old son.

On a Friday night, at 23 hours, Tina entered an aeroplane for the first time. Her amazement could not be concealed! "An aeroplane! Such a big bird! The things mzungus have discovered, mzungus are like God!" Tina exclaimed. She touched the soft clean seats with bewilderment! And the many white people on the plane, she only wished her colleagues in the bar in Malindi could just come and see how many mzungu men there were in this plane! What a waste!

I must also here mention that, before Tina left Malindi, she also made a farewell party. Most of her colleagues gave her photos

to search men for them in Germany. None of them had a specific address, but they all suggested that she could telephone or send the messages via the bar in Malindi. After all the owner, one Peter Kariuki from Karatina, knew all the girls by name.
After a acht hour flight, the Lufthansa jet landed in Frankfurt. Tina's first glimpse of Frankfurt was a wonder. What a clean city! Were there no papers in this country? How come everything seemed so clean compared to her Malindi town? Even Nairobi, though clean to Tina, could not measure up to this spotless city. She only wished that she could show her villagers how drastically her life had changed. After almost an hour of flight from Frankfurt, Tina and Bernd arrived at Berlin Tegel Airport. The size of the city was a wonder to Tina. Tina's shack hut in Malindi was no match for Bernd's beautiful apartment, too.
After a week in Berlin, Tina started to see the reality of living in Europe. Bernd now had to resume his work, and Tina had to learn to live for long hours without the only person she knew. She also realised that unlike the Germans living in Kenya, people in Berlin were not friendly. Neighbours lived like strangers and the language barrier was also a problem. All of this was compounded by the fact that Tina could only speak "street English", for she had no formal education.
Bernd left her money for use when she took her walks. What surprised Bernd was that Tina used her money extravagantly, she bought as many clothes as she could. In short, she wanted to live a life of luxury, like her many counterparts in Kenya. As luck or was it fate would have it, Tina met one Onyango from Uganda, a young man educated in Russia, but working as a dishwasher in restaurants in Berlin. Many educated immigrants from former Communist Russia have difficulties in Germany, for their education is undervalued and they end up in the unskilled labour market. This is made worse because of the German language which they have to learn to enter the job market, that costs money and is one of the many problems facing foreign intellectuals in Germany. The majority end up with manual

labour. Fortunately, the government seems to have found a solution to this and since 2005, the Immigration Office now finances an intensive language course as part of the integration. It was this Russian-educated Ugandan academic, who had turned dishwasher in Germany, who now entered Tina's life. Within a short time, an affair started between the two. Not because Tina was lonely, but because it was her way of life. Back in Malindi, every prostitute who had a white man also had a black man at the same time. Rumour had it that the white man was for money and the black man was for sex. After all, black men are famous for their sexual prowess, a factor proven by the presence of the many European women sex-tourists on the Kenyan coast. Reminds me of a chat I once had with an exchange student in Nairobi from Jamaica who said: "You go black, you never come back!".

The affair with Onyango changed both Bernd's and Tina's lives. Tina now came to meet her many ex-colleagues living and working in Berlin, started drinking heavily and had no time for Bernd. She also came to learn that she was one of the luckiest black women, since she was married to a successful German. The story is that many Germans married to foreigners are social misfits, people of dubious backgrounds, who cannot have a wife in Germany and most of them are lazy and jobless, macho, uncultured and lowly paid. Since they can't get a German woman, they end up in Kenya, Brazil, Cuba, the Caribbean Islands or Thailand, where they get poor girls with no formal education and desperate to come to Germany. A super infrastructure and governance then in Germany is almost a guarantee for every citizen to equal opportunities. So serious Germans have a good education, have no complexes, no fear of equal partners and have a free hand to choose a partner, in most cases somebody of the same status and age. Like in any society, there are also black sheep, the majority of whom turn to third world countries to look for partners. These are either notorious divorcees, playboys, people who cannot brush their teeth, obese people with a big stomach, in general social misfits, the list is end-

less. Whether it is on the beaches of Mombasa in Kenya, Phuket in Thailand or Santo Domingo in the Dominican Republic, you will find them! Pot-bellied Germans wearing massive gold chains and sandals with socks!
So for Tina to have a senior banker living in the prestigious area of Berlin-Grunewald was like hitting a jackpot. She also came to know that most Germans married to foreigners lived in cheap residential areas like Neukölln or Kreuzberg. For Tina this was news. How could a jobless person afford a ticket to Kenya? Yet many Kenyans with good salary could not even afford a flight from Nairobi to Mombasa! Little did Tina know that the German welfare system was the best in the world, and even if one was jobless, one could still save some money for a holiday. What a country!
As time went by, Tina told Bernd that she had two more children back home. To her surprise Bernd said he would bring them all to Germany, what a godsend this man was! If I remember it properly, my basic sociology taught me that a relationship is based on an equilibrium, a balance has to be there, a give-and-take formula. With Tina and Bernd, this balance was missing. It was Bernd who was giving, doing everything and Tina was only receiving, and in the long run Tina thought she was "the commander" and Bernd was the "recruit".
I must also mention here that within a month's stay in Berlin, Bernd had sent 20.000 Deutsch Marks (800,000 Kenyan Shillings) and an architectural plan for a new house to Tina's family back in Kenya. Quite a good sum of money, and within a short time, the once neglected homestead was transformed into a beautiful house, thatched with red tiles and story has it that the house remains a masterpiece in the dusty town of Tala up to this day.

The once mentioned brother of Tina took the opportunity of the purported rich German brother-in-law. He came up with an idea of starting a transport company which Bernd was willing to finance, too. In six month's time, he sent once again a check of

100.000 Deutsch Marks (4 million shillings), money given to him by his parents. Tina's remaining children in Kenya also came to Berlin. Bernd processed all the paper work, and within no time the children were admitted to German schools.
In Bernd's view, this was the beginning of a long family life and he was willing to make it a success, but little did he know that it would turn out to be a nightmare.
Tina was spending more time with Onyango, coming home late and drunk. Seven months after marrying Bernd she also claimed to be pregnant. Deep inside she was not sure whose baby it was, for she was sleeping with both Bernd and Onyango at the same time. A year after the marriage, Tina's three children were taken to a Children's Home by the Ministry of Youth and Culture. This was because many complaints had been reported by the neighbours, the children were left alone in the house for long hours and without food. Even when Tina was pregnant, she had no time for her children. To make matters worse, she told Bernd she was going to divorce him if he was not willing to share her with Onyango. Through her old mates living in Berlin Tina came to learn that white people were open in their relationships and discussed marriage problems freely with their partners. She came to learn that unlike women in Africa, if a woman in Europe cannot get sexual satisfaction from her partner, she can discuss the issue freely and she has a choice to live with him and choose a sexual partner. That such marriages exist is something African women cannot fathom to this day. In Africa, women take marriage problems like martyrs. I have a feeling that low divorce rates on the African continent have to do with the perseverance of women. High divorce rates in Nairobi support this, for the urban women are financially independent and know their rights. It is not unique to find a German couple going to bars called "Swinger Clubs", where partners swap sex mates freely to revitalise their sexual and marriage relationships. Many third world ordinary citizens living in Europe unfortunately view this equal partnership as weakness and instead of using it to harmonise their relation-

ships, they misuse it and drive their white partners into ruin! Tina even suggested that it was better for Onyango to move in and live with them. I know it sounds funny to believe, but that was Bernd's and Tina's life, he loved Tina and was willing to go to any length to make her happy, a factor she exploited mercilessly. For her, Bernd was just like any other white customer in Malindi, he got sex and he should give money for her spending and, believe me, Tina never saw anything wrong in that kind of arrangement. In winter 1985 Tina got a colored baby-boy indicating that Bernd was the father. She named him Niko, after learning that a certain man named Nikolaus brought presents during the Christmas festivities in Europe. Though a strange and new belief, Tina was ready to accept anything German without question. Reminds me of how many Kenyans embrace the idea of anything foreign, from clothes to names, accents and so forth. It still hurts me to know how christian missionaries joined hands with colonial masters to destroy African culture and tradition. They propagated the lie that our beautiful African music, dress, food and ornaments were all evil and satanic. I still feel that Africa needs a cultural renaissance. How do you explain to an African who has used a drum for centuries that it is satanic, yet the same missionaries used the drum to sing gospel music and claimed that to be different.
The colonialists really caused a lot of confusion in Africa. All the herbs our forefathers used as medicine were claimed satanic, herbs like peppermint, aloe, eucalyptus, to mention but a few, yet the same colonialists made drugs out of the same herbs and sold them to Africa, at double price, talk of double standards! What I hate most is the change of names. African names were termed as primitive and barbaric and for an African to be a christian convert, one had to have a European name! Without a European name, one could not go to heaven. The christian God only understands European, according to the European early missionaries! No wonder when I tell some Germans that my name is Theresia, they wonder and say, "really polish or catholic, how come?" They have no knowledge on the back-

ground of what their forefathers (Krapf and Rebmann) did in Africa. The practice still goes on, but to a lesser degree in countries like Nigeria and South Africa and that is why most Africans have three names, the "civilisation" name like Peter, the African birth name and the family name. The early christian missionaries knew very well that colonization of the mind was very important to reinforce the wishes of their rulers back home, and the dropping of African names was part of implementing imperialism, you know that up to this day, many Africans use European names as their gateway to heaven? Up there, the computer only identifies Europeans, otherwise you go to hell and damnation! Sadly, the modern church has done little to change this trend, yet they know very well that christianity never originated in Europe or is there a Maxwell or a Kevin in the bible?

I have now lived in Germany for ten years, and if there is something I respect the Germans for, it is their national pride. Not that I support Germans who believe that any foreigner who does not speak German is a fool, or those who think everything German is unique, I am sure most foreigners in Germany know the common phrases "German language is very hard" and "we Germans work very hard". The truth of the matter is, every language on this planet is always difficult for a non-speaker, for I believe those Germans who advocate the above will not go to Congo or Russia and speak the language overnight! How come that the majority of Germans speak"alittle English" as they say? Remember England is not far yet they are soo offended when somebody from Africa fails to spealk good German. I also believe that all over the world people work hard, irrespective of what work they do. The difference is only made by the political systems running the countries in question, sorry German puritans!, but their pride in retaining their culture I admire.

I asked myself why an African should shout at his mother for referring to him with his African name. Many young Africans prefer to be called long foreign names which are hard to pronounce by the older generation. Yet they believe being called

"Scolastica", but not "Kofi" is modern. What a mentality! Do you know that if the Africans taken as slaves to America had retained their African names, how much trouble it would have saved them to trace back their ancestry, books like "Roots" of Alex Haley would not have been written. Though judging from their looks like noses and features, it is not hard to know that the majority came from West Africa, it would have saved a lot of unanswered questions. I am not against foreign religions and cultures, but I am against people who embrace them unquestioningly. Worse still is when I see some of our people living in Europe and using dangerous skin tones to bleach themselves to become brown. Little do these people know that such creams contain poisonous agents like lead and mercury, and such substances can cause kidney failure. And who on earth told such people that looking light is beautiful? Whenever I meet such Africans in Berlin, I resist yelling at them, for they are a shame to our continent. Whoever has read a book called "Son of Lawino, Son of Okol" by the late east African professor Francis Imbuga will remember a verse in his poem about an African woman, painted with what the villagers referred to as "blood on her lips". These Africans lightening their skins are such a sight! Red face, as I would call it, looks like a rotten tomato, and black hands and legs. How the hell do you explain a multicolored skin of one individual, unless he is suffering from a skin malfunction? I don't blame the white people for calling such characters colored ("Farbige"), for they have bleached their faces which look red, yet they leave their original black color on their hands and legs. To the total black, almost blue people of Senegal and Sudan who have retained their natural complexion, I salute!

Back to our Tina. The coming of the new baby only compounded the problems in Bernd's household. What shocked Bernd most was Tina's attitude towards her children in the children's home. He anxiously waited for her to express some interest of visiting them, but all in vain. Tina demanded more money, money which Bernd could not provide as a worker. Six months

after the birth of the baby, Tina suggested to Bernd that she wanted to visit Kenya. Bernd decided to take a loan, for his savings were no more.
Back in Kenya, Tina's brother had received the check for the transport business. For sure, he had never seen a check in his lifetime and what he did was to take it to the nearest kiosk for cash. The shop keeper laughed himself silly and told the illiterate boy to take the check to a bank institute instead of a shop! With its amount, the check became the talk of Tala market.
Within a short time, the unknown boy from the poor family was now like a "mayor". Jobless school leavers from the village were now hanging around him like bees. Seeing the amount of attention he received, the boy became proud and almost drunk with power. He boasted that his sister was one of the most successful prostitutes Kenya had ever produced. Look at the transformation of his family! Wonders never cease!
When Bernd's credit check was approved, he withdrew the money and handed it all faithfully to Tina. After all, he loved this woman who had even come up with great ideas of building a villa on the beach in Kenya with minimum cost for their future. After all, Bernd did not want to spend his pension days in cold Germany.
On receiving the money, Tina shopped like a mad woman. She bought several three-piece suits for her ex-black beach boyfriend in Malindi. Talking of wrong taste, I wondered why a beach boy needed a three-piece suit in the 40° C climate of Mombasa. In any case a beach boy would have used the money better than the suit Tina bought. After her spending spree holiday in Mombasa, Tina came back to Germany and were it not for her money running out, she would have stayed longer. On her way back she cried like an oasis, claiming that she was missing her friends in Malindi. It is interesting the way human beings forget their past woes when happiness comes their way. Tina had all of a sudden forgotten the hell Bernd removed her from. Her children, though lacking parental care, had health insurance, she did not have to worry about their medical care. I

can only wonder how Tina could be so forgetful. Once she narrated to me how once in Kenya, one of her sons fell sick and unconscious. She told me about a remedy scenario that I as a Kenyan had never heard of. I quote: "One of my sons one day was very sick and unconscious, I panicked and started to cry, a coastal neighbour from the Giriama tribe screamed at me and said, "foolish woman, kojolea mtoto", meaning urinate on your child." I was flabbergasted. I had never heard of such a treatment, but Tina told me that it was a normal treatment among the coastal people, for they believed children were possessed by spirits and usually, after a mother urinated on the lifeless body, usually the children regained consciousness...! Personally, I have never experienced such an incident, but what I know is that the said area is very humid and malaria-infested, and so the chances for blood pressure ailments and malaria are high, not to mention strong traditional beliefs of spirits associated with oceanic locations! I guess mothers urinate on the children as an act of desperation.

But all this was history for Tina! During her holiday spree, she invited her own family to Mombasa. They had to share her success. Due to this reason, Tina's last holiday day in Malindi saw the police in her hotel apartment. This was because the housekeeper called the police due to a fight between Tina and her sister. Story has it that Tina's sister was demanding that she left behind her personal suitcase with all her clothes, something Tina did not want, but after all, according to the sister Tina had a rich man and therefore had no reason to bring back clothes to the land of plenty when her relatives needed them more.

I know this must sound very funny for a European, but many relatives in Africa take it as a right to own property from a relative, and the practice continues to date. It is normal for a poor man in Africa to have his fifteen children and expect the first children to finance the education of the others, for children are an investment for many poor families in Africa,. Little do these villagers know that, without formal education for their children, they are only rising future gangsters. I personally have some friends, whose fathers married a second wife and expected their now working grown-up sons to finance the education of their new half-brothers. So, German women married to our warriors, don't be surprised when they tell you that they have to send home money for the education of their half-brothers and sisters, yet their parents are living! Years back, I recall a conversation between my mother and a neighbour when I was in primary school. This woman was having her tenth pregnancy. My mother, herself a "modern parent", suggested to her friend that she should take a family planning pill. To my dismay, this woman who lived with her already nine children in a single room hut, turned down my mother's advice by saying: "I will give birth to the last egg that God gave me! After all, who knows, I might give birth to the next president. In any case, how can I take a pill without the permission of my husband." Years later I could still remember this conversation and I swear, young as I was then, I knew I never belonged to this submissive mentality. I wondered how this poor woman could expect to give birth to the next president of Kenya. And for her mentality it had to be a man. How could a man without formal education lead a country, and as a little girl then I wondered why women in Africa never saw their daughters occupying big offices. Though traditional conservative thinking, this mentality lingers on. I remember, as a television reporter back home in the 1992 multiparty campaigns I was reminded of this attitude. Gender insensitivity at its highest level. I attended a political rally in the Langata district of Nairobi. The speakers included Kenya's attorney general, then Amos Wako, and Richard Leakey, a local politician, and a young activist for KANU (yk 92). School children sung to entertain the guests, and then it was time for the donation "Harambee" to help a local school. As people gave their donations, the yk 92 activist told a ten-year-old girl who gave her donation, "Well done, little girl and mother of a future attorney general". You can imagine what I and others, advocating for equal rights in Kenya, felt. What an attitude from a young man aspiring to lead the country! He only saw a wo-

man's achievement through giving birth. He could not encourage the young girl to work hard in school and become an attorney general herself. He could only hope that she would later be "lucky" to produce a son who will take that role.
Now back to our Tina. Holiday was over and she came back to her Bernd and to Onyango. Nothing really changed, only that fights kept on breaking out in the peaceful Grunewald neighbourhood when Tina drunk one too much and Onyango exerted his chauvinistic attitudes. In all of this, Bernd's role was a passive one. For now he had realised that how much he ever tried to please Tina, nothing would "civilise" her. Once in a while, he regretted meeting a woman like her, but his love for this black beauty made him ignore the mistakes she made. He also loved his son Niko deeply and regretted that he did not spend more time with him.
The stress at home made him perform badly at work. Many summons to his head of department yielded nothing. Tina kept on drinking and inviting rowdy men and women to the apartment. Time and time again the police came to restore law and order when Tina partied with her Kenyan friends. Quarrels ranging from gossip accusations to boyfriend "snatching" or thefts were the main causes of the fights. What initially started as a friendly beer gathering, ended up in fists!
You would not have been mistaken to think Bernd's home was a Malindi Nightclub. Music was played at the highest volume! Bernd was also ashamed to tell his parents what was happening to him, for they had never approved the idea of a black daughter-in-law the first place. They still referred to their son's wife as a "nigger". They never visited from Bayern and it was hard to believe for them that their well-educated son had not married a blonde German woman. Once in a while in their farm house, they giggled when they thought of a "nigger" sleeping with their son. They knew little about African women, but they had heard that African men had big penises and were good in bed. They had also heard that the inner part of a black woman's vagina was pink instead of black. What a contrast! It was like

telling my grandmother Musaili in the village that a man can make love to a man. Unbelievable! But a reality in Europe. In Africa homosexuality is still foreign, for we do not even have a word for it. It never existed, and even if there were people with such feelings, I am sure they would never understand them, and later generations did not even have the courage to expose them. You have to understand here that an African man is supposed to be a macho, and there is no way an African man can be proud to do an act done by what he sees as a lesser being, a woman. So, it'll be wrong to imagine an African man sleeping with a man or taking the role of a woman. In my community, men tease women by asking them "Who is usually at the top in bed?" So even the sexual styles depict the male dominance and an ordinary African cannot imagine a woman on top of him in bed. In fact, many African women married to Germans see this style as an act of laziness on the man's side. It's a daily occurrence here, but a taboo in my country. It is like challenging his manhood and authority in society. The men drive and the women are the passengers! Personally I came to hear of homosexuality from my college friends from Mombasa, but then it was referred to as an "Arab and tourist practice". Homosexuality in Kenya is illegal and a top secret affair due to the discriminations and prejudices associated with it. So too are erotic videos and vibrators!

So Bernd's parents were disgusted by a "nigger" daughter-in-law, just like the way my grandmother would be to see the hundreds of men on the beach of Berlin-Wannsee, kissing and massaging each other. I cannot even imagine just telling her about an elected homosexual Major, officially opening a Gay Street Festival in Berlin! Even many Kenyans back home would only tell me that I live in Sodom and Gomorrah! Remember, the ancient biblical cities which are said to have been consumed by fire from heaven as punishment for their evil ways! In Europe we would say, maybe it was a meteorite!

As time went by, Tina seldom came home. Unlike her other three children in the children's home, Niko was always by her side. This is because she had received information from the Kenyan “rumour mills and experts” that if the last-born was taken away by the ministry and her husband divorced her, as the signs showed, then she’d be deported to Kenya. She could not imagine living in Malindi after all the grand show, worse still without money. So not because of love but for survival, Niko had to be with her in all the bars she went to.

Bernd voluntarily resigned his job and decided to go to Thailand for a holiday alone. Part of the money he received as benefits he gave Tina, who was already too happy to go back to Kenya for a holiday. As I am writing this book, Bernd is living homeless in an underground train station after spending all of his money in Thailand out of frustration.

Due to financial difficulties, Tina played the good mother and took her children from the children’s home where they were excelling, in order to get their “Kindergeld”, money given for children by the government for their upkeep. With the four children, she was entitled to get 600 Euros monthly (40 thousand shillings). The party did not last long! The atmosphere in her apartment is not conducive for education. Tina’s three children dropped out of school. Two are known gangsters in Berlin and one is rumoured to be a drug trafficker. This is not unique, a lot of children of “Safari Partners” have such an ending. The reasons are diverse. The majority of such children live in poor districts with a high crime rate, the majority of the mothers are not responsible and spend most of their time in bars. The children spend most of their time alone. Such children are very vulnerable when they are teenagers and their chances of joining gangs are high. Worse still is that the majority of the parents have never had formal education, so educational values are rarely imparted on the children when they are growing up. they grow up seeing a father who never goes to work, a drunk mother, they lack role models. The majority of colored children in Germany have a West African father, these fathers ran away after getting their resident visas. Such children too have their problems. Some of them face racism in school. What is interesting for me is that though these children are Germans, they are referred to as Africans because of their exotic features. Unlike in countries like Britain, France and America, nationality in Germany is still judged on color to a great extent. It is a common practice n the German press to refer to people as the Turkish-looking German, the German-Ethiopian... I am of the opinion that colored children are in a dilemma in this country, they are not regarded as Germans, yet they have never seen Africa. Which criteria do Germans use to define nationality? Is ignorance or could it be an indirect way of keeping racial purity? How come a mixture of two races is assumed to belong to one and not the other? Please tell me I'm wrong and give me an answer? If one is given the right to choose his nationality, that is fine, but I am against people who just look at me and ask, "where do you come from?" Amusedly, I usually answer "from Germany" and enjoy the reaction on their faces! "Ooh ... I did not eh... mean to but... where do you come from originally?"... The tragedy is that the majority of colored children born of a German women and West African men have never seen Africa with their own eyes. One cannot ignore the sense of loss of identity and its impact on such children. Put yourself in their position, you are referred to as an African, yet you are German, you have never seen Africa with your eyes, there is no positive story about the continent apart from the Safari holidays. Such children have a hard time growing up in a society where the majority of people have difficulties referring to a person of a different color as German. Their white parents also join the wagon of ignorance and tell the children that their fathers came from Africa. Some of these children, to a great extent, assume that Africa is a country like Germany. They don't know that a country like the Democratic Republic of Congo is four times bigger than Germany. They can be forgiven to believe there was only one African language. They rarely know that Africa, the cradle of mankind, has 3000 languages and 8000 dialects. Has this ignorance to do with the idea of stagnant development on the continent? I am of the opinion that all comes down to ignorance. The poor souls have only MTV singers, fashion models, Mike Tyson, basketballers and some extreme cases of illiterate drug barons driving big cars as their role models! Little do these children know that in Africa serious citizens don't have a Bob Marley-hairstyle! It is like seeing a German punk with red and blue colored shabby hair in Kenya and assuming that is how the Germans style their hair and dress! Come on, "Safari children", don't bend to these stereotypes, black or colored children can have other professions too! I know most of the living atmospheres are not conducive to learning, but where there is a will, there is a way!

As for Tina, both of her parents are dead. When Bernd's money ran out, the brother became aggressive. He kept on demanding money from the parents and when they could not give him any, he started beating them and denying them the food. The mother he threatened to rape, an insult widely believed to bring curse upon an African family. Later the father died of what Tina once narrated to me and what the doctors described as an "intestinal collapse" due to hunger. Do you know, when Tina's father died, he was laid in the most expensive mortuary in Kenya, not to mention the number of bulls slaughtered at his funeral and remember, this was a man who died of hunger! Talking of wrong priorities!. The mother later too died in Malindi under the care of Tina's nephew.

Tina's brother is now a beggar in Tala market after having sold all the furniture in the once famous house, doors and windows included! The house built by Bernd is now a white elephant and Tina still hopes to restore it one day if she marries a rich man. Her two sons were doing well in the children's home until her "Malindi" advisers told her to reclaim them so that she could receive the children support money to boost her social welfare benefits. You can guess what followed, the now organised teenage children could no longer fit in Tina's circles, tragically they have dropped out of school without a profession. I only wished that she had left them at the children's home, not the best alternative, but at least they could have completed school.

The last time I heard of them was from an elderly Kenyan man, living in Berlin, who told me that Tina had approached him to come and talk to one of her sons, for she claimed he was beating her. By doing this, Tina was still applying an African tradition that grown-ups intervene in family feuds, she was behind the time with her ideas and a stranger to her own children. In Africa, children respect any older person, be it a stranger or a relative, but not so here. From kindergarten, children are advised not to talk to strangers, let alone listen. This is due to social problems like grown-ups who rape and kill children. It is a common occurrence here. So Tina was trying to apply an African tradition to an already in Germany brought- up child, it did not work. For such children, black or colored, are Germans. In all the twenty years in Germany, Tina has never worked, never intends to and hopes "a saviour", that is rich man according to her opinion, will rescue her. Good luck, same old Tina!
The story of Tina and Bernd is a common one of a lonely German seeking love and companionship and that of a third-world inhabitant looking for the luxury and comfort that Europe can offer. Besides the natural act of sex, the partners have no common interests, no common culture, very different educational backgrounds, thus complicating the relationship even more. "Prophets of doom (sceptics)" see such relationships as warning example for a cross-continental mixed marriage. I disagree with them, for I believe good and responsible persons are found all over the world, black or white, color should not be the measure, but the normal qualities for a normal relationship.

GINA

Gina is a Kenyan girl from the Makueni district. Though Kamba by tribe, she was born and brought up in Nairobi. Her father, Mutua, was one of the successful middle-level businessmen in Nairobi down-town Gikomba, having come from the Arid Makueni district of Eastern Kenya.

As a first-born in a family of six, well-to-do by Kenyan standards, Gina went to good schools, among them the famous Makueni girls Highschool, popularly known as Unoo. Her father did the best he could to educate her, as many modern parents in Kenya do today. Gina did not have to undergo the many discriminations her age-mates in the village had to. I must state here that in many African households, parents used to opt to educate boys, in the notion that the girls would eventually marry and leave the family. A girl is seen as a passing cloud. For many fathers of Gina's age-mates, education for the boy meant prosperity for the family. However, Gina was lucky to have a father who lived in the city and was gender-conscious. Some people have always said that if you are lucky in life, you tend to take it for granted. Gina was among this group. To have luxuries like a private house on a middle-class, modest estate and a car to drop her at school, instead of being packed in morning buses like sacks of potatoes is really a luxury for many school-going children in Kenya. Instead of being grateful for that, it turned Gina into what you call a spoiled brat. She was showing off to her classmates and eventually it ended with performing poorly at Highschool grades.
However, Gina was the light of the family and her father did not fail to encourage her, even when his marriage was going through turbulent times. Due to his wealth and long hours at work, his wife had started dating young boys, something you would call "a modern wealth family syndrome" in Kenya today. This hurt the old man badly and eventually led to his death, though that's another story.
After her Highschool education, the father took Gina to a commercial college in downtown Nairobi for a course in tourism. Little did she know that the decisions that he had taken would change her life drastically. After the training, Gina secured a job with a tour company as a ticket seller. It was in this company that she met the father of her son, a renowned Nigerian drug dealer. The affair did not last long, but it exposed her to a different lifestyle. The Nigerian pampered her with money and

presents, not because of love, but because he was looking for and recruiting a future drug courier. He later rented a luxurious apartment for her, a life she was all too willing to cherish. In a nick of time she was pregnant, but little did she know that a lot was in store for her. In a flashlight, the loving Okigbo, as the Nigerian was known, changed to a womaniser and even started openly dating girls from Gina's neighbourhood. I must mention here that by now, Gina was under Okigbo's command. She was already transporting drugs via Tanzania from a small airport near Mount Kilimanjaro to South Africa, and from Nairobi to Canada and New York.

Much as she was hurt by Okigbo's behaviour, she had no way of leaving him, he used coercion and threatened to expose her to the police for being a drug courier. As she once narrated to me, the life of a drug dealer is mysterious, one morning you could wake up with one million Kenyan Shillings, that is an equivalent of 13,000 Euros, and the following week they had no money to pay the rent! So in a way she was trapped in this vicious circle of drugs and money. As time went by, the problems increased both emotionally and financially, and her pregnancy was also advancing. Due to marital problems, her father's health was also deteriorating, not to mention that by this time her mother had run away with a young Tanzanian man, to the border town of Namanga. By the time her son Tom was born, Gina contemplated committing suicide but she did not. Two months after her son was born, she decided to leave the baby with relatives and ran off to Germany. "Why Germany?" I asked her. She told me she had a cousin who was a prostitute in the famous Florida Nightclub in Nairobi and come to learn a lot about girls who married successful German men. Her cousin was living with one "nice" German and she thought she could find a better life, like many Kenyan girls living in Germany! With a drug dealer, she could not see light at the end of the tunnel and as if to confirm her fears, before she left Kenya, she got reports that Okgibo had been jailed in Europe while on his

drug transit business. As if to clean the past, Gina to this day claims Okgibo died in a road accident in Lagos!
In 1994, one spring morning, Gina landed at Tegel-Berlin Airport on board of a Lufthansa airbus from Frankfurt. At last her life was going to transform, or so she believed, in the land of opportunities. Though nobody was waiting for her, the bundle of drug dollars in her handbag gave her confidence. She was sure to get a nice hotel and later start her search for the hoped rich German Prince Charming! Little did she know that a lot waited in store for her. She managed to book herself a room at the Ibis Hotel near the famous International Exhibition Centre in Berlin-Charlottenburg. I must mention here that Gina is a very talkative girl, a fact that helped her in the days to come.
The following day, she took a walk in the famous Kurfürstendamm Street, popularly known as Ku-Damm and frequented by tourists. It is here where she met the one man who would introduce her to Berlin life and the Kenyan community in Berlin. The man is one Wekesa from the Kakamega district of Kenya. Though illiterate, Wekesa knows his way around. He was once a famous beach boy in Mombasa where he met his old German wife who brought him to Berlin. Little did he know that his sexual prowess would earn him a name in the then West-Berlin. In no time he realised that his sexual prowess was a tool which not only earned him a marriage certificate and residence in Germany, but a living standard he could only dream of as a beach boy in Bamburi. He also realised that he could divorce the old granny "Oma" and marry a sweet young girl. To cut a long story short, Wekesa came to know a lot of German women who loved black men. They spoiled him with luxuries, including presents and trips exclusive holiday resorts, even to the rich principality of Monaco, call it a dream come true! It is hard to believe, but this lifestyle gave Wekesa so much confidence that he started believing that he was a "superman" who could even show around Kenyan intellectuals and politicians visiting Berlin. In other words, he proclaimed himself to visiting Kenyans as the unofficial Kenyan ambassador and president in Germany.

So you can be sure when Gina met Wekesa in Ku-Damm, she was in the "right hands!" In no time he had suggested that she could move in with him in his "villa", a four-bedroomed apartment in the Schöneberg district, an offer which was too good to deny. I must mention here that Wekesa, illiterate as he might be, was very "clever" in his world and he had learned with time not to let an opportunity pass by. For Wekesa it was a glorious opportunity to meet a homeless, new and young black woman, willing to go and live in his apartment. By this time Wekesa was separated from his young German wife and mother of his two sons.

While Gina was living with Wekesa, he got her a job, of course illegal, in a discotheque. Though poorly paid, the 1.000 marks then (40,000 shillings) she was earning was good money for Kenyan standards. Wekesa had the idea of putting a partner search advertisement in one of the city magazines, "tip". To her amazement, Gina got over fifty letters, one of which changed her life. The letter was from a German mechanical engineer named David. He was thirty-five years old and was working with a famous Germany car company. To Gina this was a dream come true, first an educated young man and rich by German standards.

In no time Gina was in "love", not in the real sense of the word, but she saw an opportunity to live well in Germany. In no time she convinced David for marriage, for her stay in Germany was soon going to be illegal. As a tourist from Kenya then she was only allowed to live here for three months without a visa, so by marrying him she would secure her stay. I should state here that besides the good salary David was earning, he also had two private houses and a collection of five cars, among them two oldtimers, not a bad "catch" for a "gold digging woman".

Within a month's meeting Gina made sure she convinced David for marriage. After all, David was glad to have a partner in this lonely city, Berlin being popularly known for its single population. Loneliness is like a pest in the city and one considers oneself lucky if one finds a partner. All the same, David, as many

other Germans, was sceptical about marrying a foreigner. Many Germans had fallen victims of “paper marriage”. These are marriages between Germans and foreign opportunists who use the marital status to secure residence and enjoy the good German infrastructure. Popular examples of such marriage partners come from the former eastern European countries, West Africa, Thailand and South America. When David expressed his fears, Gina assured him that she loved him genuinely. However, David sought advice from a lawyer to marry Gina on a marriage contract. I must mention here that due to many complaints and loss of property, the German government allows one to marry with a contract that in the event of divorce, the partners do not take financial advantage and claim the property owned by the financially stable partner before their marriage. This too includes property inherited from parents. Gina had no alternative but to keep a brave face and convince David that she was not interested in his earthly possessions! A bitter pill to swallow, but they say a bird in the hand is better than two in the bush!
A marriage date was set and both travelled to Kenya where marriage bureaucratic procedures were less complicated than in Germany. Rumour from Gina’s relatives has is that before the marriage ceremony took place at Sheria House, she literally “locked” David in the house and no relatives except her sisters and brother were allowed to see him, the reason being that she was scared he might change his mind on seeing other beautiful Kenyan women.
After the marriage, Gina took her now one year old son to Berlin, to a life of comfort, as many believed. On arrival the spoiled Gina arranged a party, the chief coordinator being no other than Wekesa. Rumour has it that Wekesa mobilised literally all the Kenyans living in Berlin for the party, with the aim of showing them how he had helped a Kenyan to secure a rich German. After all everybody knew that Gina had lived in Wekesa’s apartment and that her success was Wekesa’s doing.
The party date was a Saturday and this is a day Gina will never forget due to the events that followed. To David’s shock, over

fifty Kenyans arrived in his small house compound. Of interest to note is that David's house was a moderate fifty square-meter house, but not a villa. All the same this was enough reason for Gina to show off to her countrymen, since most of them were living in small rooms, not to mention the majority living in refugee camps in the Eastern part of Berlin.

The big number of the guests was one reason to raise David's temper. Not to mention that they never came with a bottle to assist the party as it is the custom here. As with the Germans, unlike Africans, when one is annoyed, you don't wait until the visitors go. David declared his unhappiness on the spot by not greeting any of them, for an African this is a major insult to hospitality. To add injury to insult, David told the party revellers that they should vacate his compound by five o'clock for he needed his peace, "Ruhe". This really embarrassed Gina and Wekesa, but as usual, they had a solution and an answer for everything that happened to a Kenyan living in Germany. "You people enjoy yourselves and forget about these Germans", said Wekesa. "After all, ask me, I have lived here for over ten years and I know what kind of people they are. They are used to living alone, no visitors and do not know communal living", added Wekesa.

A drunk party-goer, Kuria by name, added: "After all look at the many dogs in the streets, they prefer to rear animals than living with people, they even put their parents in care homes while they are busy working and buying good comfortable cars for their dogs!" "Do you know, you guys, that Germans have expensive dog and cat hair salons? And Berlin even has a five star hotel for canines!" added Veronica. " There are even animal cemeteries, decorated with flowers by professional gardeners!" Everyone cheered and laughed at the big cultural differences.

The party went on, but Gina knew there would be no peace after it. True to his word and against the wishes of the majority, David ordered the drunk Kenyans out of his compound at five o'clock. You can imagine the gossip that followed, the philosophies and the opinions on cultural differences between Germans and Africans. It is unfortunate that such relationships are victims of false judgements and opinions. I must also state here that, despite the problems Africans face in Germany, very few of them, if any, have the courage to tell their people back home about them and in a way this is one of the reasons I am writing this book. In their manual jobs with little income, a year's savings can afford them a holiday back home, thus giving the impression that they are rich in Germany.

In a way I agree with many that Germany is a paradise. Consider a poor prostitute waiting for tourists in the streets of Nairobi. What she earns can barely pay a one-room rent in Huruma estate with a communal toilet. The same holds true for the beach-boys in Mombasa. When such people come to Germany, they can at least live in a good apartment, the likes of Kilimani or Kizingo style in both Nairobi and Mombasa. They can save the money they earn from washing dishes. At least a month's income of 800 Euros (80,000 Ksh) is not bad for Kenyan standards, if you understand what I mean! The welfare system too. A jobless single safari partner divorcee (most of them are) with four children gets a government upkeep allowance of the equivalent of half a million Kenyan shillings! Mind you, an executive salary in Kenya! So, the dream lives on, wealth made in Germany! Back to my Gina.

After the "crowd" had left, as David kept on calling the Kenyans, Gina now faced the reality of a mixed marriage. Her marriage was really mixed in terms of color, culture, common interests, intellectuality and so on. According to Gina, things went from bad to worse. On Gina's invitation I also managed to talk to David and his opinion was not better. He lamented to me that he was married to a stranger. Up to now I do not know why David confided to me. He said he was not a racist, but he found Gina too extreme and difficult to understand. In general they had nothing in common. In my opinion, Gina, unlike many of her country folk, was informed, confident, stubborn and egoistic. On the other hand, David was frustrated, for in my opinion

Gina did not fit into his "plan" of a wife. He saw her as a part of his collections, just like his wines in the cellar and the fleet of cars he owned. Unlike the car he could command, Gina, his exotic collection, did not obey him! And this was her crime. He did not marry an independently thinking German woman, for she would not fit into his "Yes, sir"- collection, he thought an African immigrant would, he was wrong! You can say he got a white independent with a black skin and that spelled trouble. At one time he yelled at her when she refused to clean his house, boldly telling him that she was not his cleaning woman. Bitterly he yelled at her and said, "Nigger, if I needed a wife I would have married a German woman." Gina's self-confidence was a threat to David's world, although he was educated. Such men like David are found in the western world too, men who want a submissive wife in modern Europe, men who feel deprived of their powerful social role. The lucky ones end up marrying poor third world immigrants looking for survival in western Europe. The unlucky ones like David end up with self- confident middle- class immigrants. It is an impossible cocktail which ends up breaking the glass. I once had a chat with a Kenyan lady student, who remarked that it was hard for an educated African woman to get a husband in Germany and this has its reasons. Men who like black women do not look for independent thinkers, otherwise they would have married their country women. They suffer from low self-esteem and look for "dolls" whom they can mould and advise to boost their ego. It is just like back home in Kenya where some educated men avoid to marry women of their cadre, with the claim that they are too "bigheaded" and in any home only one person can wear the trousers! This scores the fear of an independently thinking woman, it threatens the core of the male macho and the traditional role played by men. A hundred years ago, women in Europe won this war, unfortunately there are still remnants of men who still don't come to terms with it and instead they look for uninformed, timid and poor women from third world countries.

What followed after the summer party was disaster. David decided that his only television set was better off with his parents in Frankfurt. This was because according to him, Gina and her son spent their whole day glued to television, a behaviour he found primitive and irritating. The following winter, he also shut down all the heating system in his house, something that led to sickness for Gina and her son. Mind you, the winter is sometimes minus 15°C, too extreme for a person coming from tropical Africa. David claimed that the heating system was too expensive. He did all these things due to the stressful situation at home. These events spread like bush fire among the Kenyan community in Berlin, thanks to Gina and Wekesa, the veteran.
To add injury to insult, David moved from the matrimonial bed and even declared to Gina that marrying a stubborn African woman was the biggest mistake of his lifetime. After all he claimed that his love had always been for blond women! Talking of being blind, surely this amused me, because a person who loves blond women must have been blind and crazy to marry a black woman! Talk of African charms and wizardry at its best!
One year after their marriage, Gina decided to look for a job, since David did not give her pocket money despite the tax deductions he got due to his new marital status. No normal German, intellectual or manual worker, treats his wife like this. The law provides that a housewife should have an allowance! David knew that very well, but he exploited Gina's foreign status and financial insecurity mercilessly. She got small jobs in private homes, like ironing and making beds in hotels. But this kind of financial independence did not help the relationship in the house. She was also getting "Kindergeld" (150 Euros monthly) for her son, money given by the state to every child to assist in its upbringing.
Like many of our counterparts in Germany, Gina was torn between pride and survival. After all she had paraded a rich German in front of her relatives after the marriage and she had to live up to the show! An expensive and trying show. Her mother

expected her to telephone home every week and that costs money. She made secret calls, in the hope that the husband would not notice and complain. To her shock the telephone bill shot from the normal one hundred marks David used to have to a thousand marks. You can imagine the chaos it caused. David reacted violently and plucked the telephone and threw it in the cellar. If only that could have altered the figures! Quarrels and lectures followed, and David decided forthwith not to have a telephone in the house. I personally pay my bills and I understand the cause of his anger, but to Gina and her gang this was just a "mean German" who did not understand the value of extended families and relatives in Africa! After all, how could Gina stop her mother from telling her on the telephone over an hour how the cows were healthy and how the El Nino rains had ruined their Kaiti farm, an important discussion for an African family, but irrelevant and difficult for a German to understand. Whereas Africans in such telephone conversations are emotionally bound by family units and bonds, westerners tend to think more on the financial implications of such long calls and in their opinion unnecessary conversations!

Things moved from bad to worse. David stopped talking to Gina and her son. Sometimes it pained me to see the two- year-old greet "uncle David", as he usually called him, to no response. In Africa where I come from, grown-ups have differences, they differ, it is normal in a relationship to disagree, but however strong the differences are, children are never involved. We might fight, but when I meet a child, I will say "good morning" with a smiling face, it is pretence but we culturally believe it is a constructive pretence. Children are not supposed to be involved in adult affairs. Many communities in Kenya advise newly-weds to always lock their bedrooms when they are quarrelling to protect the children.

To make matters worse, David now bought his own separate food. The nightmare was that they still had to share the same kitchen and refrigerator. But you know what: he wrote his name on the food products, including each egg and can of yoghurt. I

swear, for an African this is too extreme, but for some people here it is normal to write names on eggs. I experienced it too, when I moved to the Frauenhaus. One of my many culture shocks!
One day I saw something that I'll never forget. Gina had invited me for a chat. Around four o'clock David came home from work, never said "hallo" to any of us and went to the kitchen. What followed next will always remain a "scream". He screamed at the top of his voice and my first instinctive reaction was that the small boy had hurt himself, for he was crying too. I ran with Gina to the kitchen and found the 35 year old engineer holding the neck of the two year old boy, shaking him and screaming at the top of his voice. I asked him what was wrong and he replied: "Tell your bastard that he is not supposed to touch my yoghurt. If you people where you come from can't read and write, you'd better signal to your son where your cheap food products are stocked."
I had no words. Honestly, my legs wobbled, and I did not want to believe what I saw and heard, what was really happening in front of my eyes. I immediately told Gina to dress her son and accompany me to a nearby park for some talk and peace. I honestly told Gina to leave this man if she loved her son. This was no environment to bring up a child. To my amazement, Gina decided to stay and to make matters worse. She even told her Kenyan "jury" in Berlin that I was jealous of her lifestyle. She claimed she had an educated man, rich and I did not have one. After all I was more educated than her, yet I did not have "a quality man" like her. I gave up. I have always blamed myself for thinking that I could save and change people's lives. I seem to suffer from what I jokingly refer to as my "Mother Theresa syndrome". Unfortunately it is something in me, it makes me happy and sometimes it is costly, but I seem to repeat the same mistakes all the time. Before I gave up on Gina, I advised her once again to leave David early enough. The foreign law in Germany sates that if one marries a foreigner, you don't get a resident visa until after a three-year spell. Gina had a three-year

visa, but her permanent residence visa could only be obtained when her spouse accompanied her to the migration office after the completion of the three years. Discriminating as the law sounds, it protects German citizens from unscrupulous asylum seekers and I believe it is justified, for the duty of any government is to protect its citizens. I advised Gina to leave David early enough when she still had time to look for another man, sounds unscrupulous but reasonable enough if you've become a victim of foreign law statutes.

I swear, I never learn. She repeated the same gossip to her "jury" and for the last time I promised myself not to involve myself in Kenyan affairs in Berlin. How long I would stick to this promise, only time would tell!

Three years later, on a spring morning, I was taking a walk on the Schlossstraße in the district of Steglitz by coincidence. I saw Gina walking in the same vicinity. We greeted each other well as if there had been no differences between us before. As usual, she narrated her chaotic life with David and apologised for our last misunderstanding. Naive as I have always been, little did I know that she was looking for help. She finally requested me to help her get a good lawyer, for David had issued her with a legal notice to vacate his house. I asked her more on the issue, but she told me it all had started with a bottle of wine! Interesting, but not surprising to believe. According to Gina, one of her younger sisters from Nairobi had visited her that summer with her Italian boyfriend. As always, she pretended her life was normal, went to David's cellar and got some wines for her guests. Luckily enough, David had gone to Stuttgart for a meeting. Unexpectedly he came back and found Gina and her guests, never greeted them and as fate would have it, he proceeded to the cellar. How unfortunate! What followed is everybody's guess. He burst into the living-room, screamed at the top of his voice and asked Gina who had given her the right to go into his cellar. To the amazement of the Italian guest he said: "Nobody in this house is supposed to touch the wines in my cellar. Those are special wines, meant for me and my brothers, especially reserved for we take them yearly to celebrate our singlehood."

I was shocked. My own analysis was that David was or believed he was single, which then meant there was never a marriage known to his relatives. So either he was living in a lie, or Gina had told us a lie, after all the notice to leave the house coincided with the three years' of marriage, which meant this was a "contract marriage" and the African in Gina kept her hoping that David would change his mind and live with her for good. His "singlehood" remark could only mean that he married Gina, like many other Germans did, to save money with tax deductions and for sure, in three years he must have saved some amount! Time and time again I wondered what might have gone wrong with the marriage "agreement", if at all it existed. Disappointments lead to bitterness and sometimes costly results. What was more hurting, he never accompanied her to the migration office and that meant no resident visa for Gina, three years lost, psychological torture and shattered dreams. One early morning Gina stole David's identity card to go and obtain a permanent residence visa to the amazement of the immigration officers. She hoped that the identity card would help her get the visa. In clear words the immigration officer told Gina to go and bring her spouse as required by law. Poor Gina!

Divorce was not the only trouble ahead. She had secured a loan for her driving lessons and a second hand old car, her employer had sacked her before she could pay back her loan fully, no job, no income, no apartment and no resident visa, a tough life with hard choices to make. The only alternative for Gina now was to go to the Frauenhaus, a house set by organisations to help abused women in distress, a good and noble project, and, believe me, it has not only helped German women but even more foreign women.

The other alternative Gina had was to grab the next German man and get a baby. Sounds like a joke and crafty but it happens, for if she conceived, it was a sure way of eliminating deportation! Life is not a straight line or so they say.

The Mother Theresa in me was ticking. I gave Gina an address of a Frauenhaus in Berlin-Kreuzberg and an advocate's address, too. I also advised her to look for a job before her divorce. With the period of time she was married, she was eligible to a permanent residence if she could prove to earn her own living and not depend on social welfare. As I am writing this book, Gina has left the Frauenhaus, waiting for her divorce proceedings. In Germany, divorce proceedings take place after one year of separation. Gina also has a new baby-girl, conceived in a disco toilet as she proudly tells people. Life has hardened her and even if this man does not marry Gina, the child will be a sure way and ticket to keep her in Germany by law. They say in my language: "Asiyefunzwa na Mamaye hufunzwa na Uliwengu", meaning whoever is not taught by their mother is taught by the world. An unfair way to use a child for existence and survival, but after all, who said life was fair?

GLOSSARY

Jambo	hello
Karibu	Welcome
Jina	name
Daktari	Doctor
Askari	soldier/policeman
Kwaheri	goodbye
Lala Salama	good night
Maji	water
Matiti	breasts
Hakuna matata	no problem
Mzungu	European / white person
Msafiri	traveller
Malaya	prostitute
Nyama choma	barbecue
Simba	lion
Ulaya	Europe
Safari	journey

KISWAHILI SAYINGS

1. Asiyefunzwa na Mamaye hufunzwa na Ulimwengu – He who is not taught by his mother is taught by the world.
2. Asiyetembea hufikiri mamaye ni Mpishi – He who has never travelled thinks his mother is the best cook.
3. Mgeni ni Mbaraka – A visitor brings blessings.
4. Mtaka cha Mvunguni sharti ainame – He who wants something from the floor must bend.
5. Kuishi kwingi ni kuona mengi - He who lives long experiences more.
6. Mpanda ngazi hushuka – He who climbs comes down; meaning pride comes before a fall, humility is important.
7. Msafiri ndiye mwenya tobako kali – He who travels has the best tobacco

About the author

Terri Muvanya-Wishmann was born in 1964 in Machakos, Kenya.
She attended Tumu Tumu Girls high school, and graduated in 1989 with a Bachelor of Arts degree (B:A Hons) in Sociology from the University of Nairobi. She is a holder of a post-graduate Diploma in Journalism.
Before migrating to Germany in 1997 Terri worked in Nairobi as a television News Reporter and Editor. She lives with her son today in Berlin-Zehlendorf. She is a correspondent for a German Radio station and a founder of an Aids Orphans home in Kenya.